Spinsters, Spies, and Murder

Victoria Parker Regency Mysteries

Book 5

Jennifer Monroe

Copyright © 2021 Jennifer Monroe

All rights reserved.

This book is a work of fiction. Names, characters, businesses, places, events and incidents are either the products of the author's imagination or used in a fictitious manner. Any resemblance to actual persons, living or dead, or actual events is purely coincidental.

Victoria Parker Regency Mysteries Series

Dukes, Drinks, and Murder

Captains, Lies, and Murder

Brides, Blackmail, and Murder

Marquesses, Muskets, and Murder

Spinsters, Spies, and Murder

Duchesses, Diamonds, and Murder

Chapter One

Miss Victoria Parker, better known as Vicky by those closest to her, watched with interest the interview that was taking place at her accounting firm. Mr. James Kensington, her associate and the man with whom she had developed a close relationship, sat at the large oak desk that had once belonged to her father. James had taken over her father's position after his death, or at least appeared to have done so; few clients would have accepted a woman as the person to balance their books, after all.

Across from James sat Mr. Andrew Thompson, a thin, quiet yet nervous man of two and twenty years who was interviewing for the new accountant position within the firm. He had wire-rimmed spectacles and what appeared to be an attempt at a mustache on his upper lip, although it needed time to become anything substantial.

They had interviewed three potential candidates, and Mr. Thompson had proven to be the best fit thus far. The other two applicants seemed knowledgeable and had far more experience than Mr. Thompson, but they also had telltale facial lines indicating an irascibility that likely made them men with whom it would be difficult to work. Not to mention the fact that they would likely balk at having Vicky as their employer.

"Most days we leave for home in the late afternoon – no later than five on any typical day," James was explaining. "There are times, however, when we may need to work much later, perhaps even as late as eight or nine. Will this be a problem for you?"

"No!" Andrew blurted and then leaned back in his chair and took a deep breath. "Forgive me. What I mean to say is that I am able to work as late as is necessary. Mr. Fitzsimmons, who oversaw my internship, can swear by my work ethic and my ability to change as the circumstances warrant it."

Vicky walked over to the small desk that rested beneath a window looking out onto Wellington Street. Beside it sat a bookcase that housed a collection of ledgers, most belonging to their clients. She took a seat and listened further.

Mr. Thompson adjusted his glasses as beads of sweat dotted his forehead. His breath came in short gasps, and he pulled at the cravat around his neck.

James had asked him every conceivable question, and the young man had answered all with earnest. Vicky sensed something very good about him, and she was certain he would make a fine addition to the firm. If he did not faint from fright first.

"Is there anything you would like to add, Miss Parker?" James asked. They had agreed to address one another formally until their new employee had settled in a bit. Their blooming romance did not need to be revealed for the time being.

"Indeed, I do have a question," Vicky said. She did not miss how the man's hands trembled in his lap. "Across the street is a young lady who has been watching our office. Can I assume that you are acquainted with her?"

Mr. Thompson nodded and a blond wave fell over his brow. "Yes, Miss Parker, that would be my wife, Jenny. She accompanied me here today to give me a bit of encouragement."

Vicky glanced at James, who gave a tiny nod. Mr. Thompson's face reddened to his ears as he rushed on to add, "I can assure you that if you hire me, she will not bother you or Mr. Kensington. We have already arranged where to meet for our midday meal every day, but she will not be in the way, nor will she be bothering me while I am working.

And if you prefer that she not be in the office at all, that can easily be arranged. It is just that we have not been married long and we tend to enjoy each other's company..." He clamped his mouth shut as if he had said too much.

Vicky smiled. This man was exactly who the firm needed. He was kind, soft-spoken – when he was not rushing his words – and possessed all the qualities necessary to do his job.

"Well," Vicky said as she stood, "I suggest you inform her that if she wishes to join you for any meal, she is more than welcome to come inside. I see no reason to have her waiting for you elsewhere. After all, we cannot have her standing outside, now can we? Not when the London weather can be so unpredictable."

Mr. Thompson's eyes widened. "Did I hear you correctly?" he asked, his voice trembling. "Are you saying I have the position?"

"Indeed," Vicky replied. "Welcome to Parker Accounting. Now, if you would like, invite your wife to come inside so she may see your new place of employment."

Mr. Thompson stood, nearly toppling over his chair in his hurry. He had to grasp hold of the edge of the desk to steady himself as he wiped his brow. "I cannot express how thankful I am for this opportunity," he said, taking the hand James offered him and pumping it vigorously. "I will go and get Jenny and tell her the wonderful news!"

With hurried steps, he left the office, the door in the vestibule closing with a loud *bang!*

Vicky laughed. "There is no doubt that he will fit in quite well here," she told James. "I am glad he will be joining us. You were so right to recommend him."

With the acquisition of the accounts belonging to the Lenthurst brothers, a formidable addition to their client list, Parker Accounting was growing faster than two accountants could handle. After several heated discussions – or rather arguments – James had convinced Vicky that a new accountant would be not only advisable but also necessary.

James had spent a great deal of time shuffling through paperwork, setting aside information given about those who lacked the proper training or those who came without references. Some even came with references that when James spoke to them, they advised against employment for various reasons, some quite shocking. She was surprised that, by the end, he could only recommend they interview the three out of more than two dozen.

The main reason Vicky had been against bringing in someone new was that by doing so, the firm that had belonged to her father would change. She wanted it to remain as it was when he was alive. It took many months for her to realize that everything in life changes and would continue to do so whether she liked it or not. She finally came to the realization that they had no choice if she wished to continue with the level of professionalism they had always been able to offer their clients.

She glanced at James, and her heart overflowed. The fact the man who suggested to her who they should hire was a close friend and business associate – and now the man she loved – helped a great deal in her decision.

"Now that Mr. Thompson will be joining us," James said, "you will have more time to spend with Percy. Or anything else that may need your attention."

Percy Lock was a young boy of nine that every shopkeeper on Wellington Street knew quite well. He had spent a great deal of his younger years running errands and taking home a few coppers as often as he could. His mother, Julia, had left the boy in Vicky's care while she went to visit her ill sister. A month later, she informed Vicky she no longer wanted the boy.

Vicky had gladly taken on Percy to raise him as her own. And with the help of James over the past six weeks, she had done just that.

"Having Mr. Thompson here will provide time for both of us," Vicky said with a smile. The front door opened, and she lowered her voice. "But do not use the new help as an excuse to become lazy, Mr. Kensington, or I shall dock your wages until you are receiving nothing more than three pieces of coal per week!" She added a wink, which made James laugh.

Their shared banter began not long after James first joined the firm years ago, oftentimes encouraged by – and in participation with – her father. Yet as their friendship turned into something more, it had become all the more playful.

"If I talk too much," Vicky overheard Mr. Thompson whisper to his wife, "nudge me with your elbow. I do not want to lose this opportunity before it even begins!"

The couple appeared at the doorway between the vestibule and the office. Mrs. Thompson was around the same age as her husband, with rosy cheeks, dark hair, and deep blue eyes that matched the printed flowers on her dress.

"Oh, do stop worrying," his wife returned in as quiet a voice. "And do keep your apologizing to a minimum. You do not want to annoy them, now, do you? Do not forget what Mr. Fitzsimmons told you. He was quite clear with what you needed to improve on, and none of his suggestions had anything to do with your accounting abilities." She smiled at him and straightened his cravat. "But do not worry, I have every faith in you."

"Sorry," Mr. Thompson murmured before covering his mouth.

Upon seeing Vicky and James staring at them, Mrs. Thompson's eyes went wide, and she nudged her husband.

He turned around. "Oh, Miss Parker, Mr. Kensington. I did not see you there."

Vicky wondered if he wore a permanent blush as she smiled and said, "Unless you have eyes in the back of your head, I imagine you would not."

Mrs. Thompson grinned, and Vicky suspected that they would get on well.

"Well, introduce me," Mrs. Thompson whispered.

"Oh, yes, right," Mr. Thompson said, his face reddening further, if that were possible. "Miss Parker, Mr. Kensington, this is my wife, Mrs. Jenny Thompson."

"It is a pleasure to meet you, Mrs. Thompson," Vicky said.

It was Mrs. Thompson's turn to blush. "The pleasure is all mine."

"Allow me to show you where you will be working," James said. "Miss Parker recently refurbished the room."

Initially, she had been resistant to the change; after all, the extra room was filled with memories of her father. Yet, after much urging from James, she had cleared out what was no longer needed. Gone were the stacks of clothing, books she was certain no one would read, and several crates of bits and bobs her father had refused to get rid of when he was alive. It had been a heart-wrenching task, but once it was completed, she was left with a strange sense of relief. Removing those items had not wiped away the memories of her father, which had been her greatest fear.

"I have left the bookcase empty so you may use it as you wish," Vicky said. "I hope you do not mind the paintings. My father enjoyed them, so I thought I would hang them here, but if you would prefer—"

"They are lovely," Mrs. Thompson said, walking over to touch the canvas that depicted a meadow filled with wildflowers. "I am sure my husband will be pleased with them, will you not, my dear?"

Her husband gave a vigorous nod. "They are lovely," he said, smiling. "It is nice to have a bit of nature to look at while I am working, as there are no windows." His eyes went wide again, and he quickly added, "Not that I am complaining, mind you. I get enough nature when I am out and about." He closed his eyes for a moment, took a deep breath, and then asked, "Would you like me to begin today?"

James shook his head. "I suggest you begin on Monday. Enjoy a quiet weekend with your wife without having any accounts grinding in your mind. Where is it you live again?"

"Pembroke Street," Mr. Thompson replied.

"Pembroke?" James asked, his brows raised. "Are you acquainted with Mr. Gregory Langley?"

Mr. Thompson nodded. "I believe so. Does he not own the house on the corner of...?"

As the two men continued their conversation, Vicky touched Mrs. Thompson on the arm and led her into the other room. "Men tend to talk for hours," she said with a laugh. "Would you like a cup of tea?"

"Oh, no, thank you, Miss Parker," Mrs. Thompson replied. "You have a beautiful office. I have never met a woman who has a business with her name on it, unless she has a boarding house or finishing school. How wonderful for you!"

Vicky laughed. "Parker Accounting once belonged to my father," she explained as she offered the woman a chair. "It is his name on the firm, not mine. When he died, Mr. Kensington took on the role of head accountant, but just between you and me," she glanced around the room and lowered her voice, "that is merely for the sake of the business. If any of our clients knew I was in charge of their finances, they would flee in terror and leave us bankrupt by the morning."

"Well, I, for one, believe women should own businesses," Mrs. Thompson said with a firm nod. "One day, I will open a millinery, though I know not the first thing about how to run any type of establishment. But I do like hats." She heaved a sigh. "Andrew supports my dream, and that is why I love him so much."

For a moment, Vicky thought of James and understood what Mrs. Thompson meant. Life was difficult enough facing it alone, but when a person has someone who supports them and is willing to face those difficulties together, it makes it that much easier.

"As an accountant," Vicky replied, "your husband will be just the right person to help you. If you are able to focus on the hats and he on the accounting, I believe you will find much success. I would recommend – if you lack the skills to do so on your own, of course; I do not wish to make any assumptions – but I do suggest that he teach you how to manage your daily accounts. The most successful shops employ an accountant to maintain the overall ledgers, so the proprietors can focus on giving their clients the best service possible."

Mrs. Thompson smiled. "I appreciate the advice."

"Jenny," Mr. Thompson said as he and James entered the room, "I think we can go now. Unless you need me to do anything, Mr. Kensington. I do not mind."

James shook his head. "Not at the moment."

"Miss Parker?"

Vicky stifled a chuckle. The man was certainly persistent. "As Mr. Kensington mentioned earlier, you will begin on Monday."

Mrs. Thompson sighed. "That means it is time for us to go, dear."

"Oh, yes, of course," her husband said. "My apologies."

Vicky and James followed the couple to the front door and bade them farewell.

"Parker Accounting has a new employee," James said as he closed the door. "Tell me, how does it feel, Miss Parker?"

Vicky turned to face him. "Wonderful," she replied. "And a relief. Mr. Thompson is a bright young man and his wife is lovely. I think he will fit in quite well here."

"I could not agree more," James said. He brushed back a wave of dark hair that had fallen across his brow. As it happened of late, Vicky's heart fluttered with overwhelming desire to be held by him. They had promised to remain dignified while the firm was in operation during the day, but at times such as this, a simple kiss was all too tempting.

"I believe I will invite him to have an ale with me after we finish work on Monday," James said.

Vicky clicked a playful tongue at him. "I would prefer you did not teach him your bad habits, Mr. Kensington," she said, poking his chest with a finger, although she could not have called up even one habit that she did not already adore.

Chapter Two

A knock made her start, and when Vicky opened the door, she found Percy accompanied by a gentleman in a fine coat.

"Hi, Miss Vicky," Percy said with a dramatic sigh. As usual, his cheeks were covered in dirt, as were his hands. "This 'ere's Mr. Footman."

The man's face darkened. "It is Butler," he snapped. "Mister David Butler, director of the Easterling Art Gallery."

Vicky had heard of the gallery, although she had never had the pleasure of visiting it. She understood that it exhibited fine art by famous painters from all over England as well as a few from Paris but otherwise knew nothing more about it.

"May we speak for a moment concerning this young lad?" Mr. Butler asked.

Percy lowered his gaze.

What kind of trouble has he gotten himself into this time? Vicky wondered. It was not that Percy was mischievous, not on purpose. At times, he simply became too inquisitive for his own good.

Vicky invited Mr. Butler into the office and offered him a chair. The man removed his hat to reveal dark hair that had been combed to a single large curl on top of his head. He touched his heavy sideburns often, as if to ascertain they were still there. His blue coat was finely tailored, and his boots shone to a high sheen. With a nose much too large for his face and a mouth twisted in a permanent scowl, he was not a handsome man by any stretch of the imagination.

James sat at the large desk, and Vicky stood beside the bookcase, her hands on Percy's shoulders. What had the boy been up to this time? He had never been a thief, nor did he intentionally cause trouble, but young boys were curious, and Percy was no exception. Thoughts of a torn canvas or a shattered sculpture came to mind. What were works of art valued at these days? Certainly tens, if not hundreds or thousands, of pounds. Where would she find that kind of money if she were asked to pay for damages?

"I understand that you are guardians to this young man," Mr. Butler said.

"We are," James replied. "Or rather Miss Parker is. I am employed by the accounting firm and therefore shoulder some of the responsibility. May I ask what happened? Did Percy damage something at the gallery?"

Mr. Butler, who sat on the very edge of the chair with a back as stiff as a board, said, "We at the Easterling Art Gallery hosted an early exhibition this morning for the...let us say, healthier endowed members of the aristocracy. They came from near and far to see the newest pieces by a local artist who has become quite popular as of late. Mr. Leslie Billingsly? Surely you have heard of him?"

Vicky glanced at James, who returned her blank expression. "I am afraid we have not, Mr. Butler. But please, go on."

"Of course you are not," the man said with a curled lip. "Those of the...excuse the expression but those of lesser means are not as likely to be familiar with the contemporary artists."

"And what did Percy do exactly, Mr. Butler?" James asked, tiny spots of red splashing his cheeks. Vicky understood his reaction; just because someone asks to be excused for giving offense does not necessarily remove the sting.

"All was going well during the exhibition until this boy," he gestured toward Percy, "entered the gallery and disrupted the proceedings."

"Disrupted how exactly?" James asked. "Percy, what did you do?"

Percy dropped his gaze and replied, "I didn't know the ladies'd scream. All I did was show 'em me frogs I'd caught. They were the biggest and bestest frogs I'd ever gotten and I wanted to show 'em off."

Vicky closed her eyes in embarrassment, imagining the scene unfolding as Mr. Butler continued, "I am uncertain how the boy gained entry into the gallery, but what I do know is that Lady Malkins fainted, Miss Rose Albright screamed in terror, nearly knocking over a nearby work, and Lord Greene vowed never to return to the gallery! I have never witnessed such a spectacle in all my life. The gallery is meant to be a place where those of means may go and enjoy themselves without such incidents taking place. Now I fear our name will be ruined forever."

James turned a stern glare on Percy. "Is this true?"

Percy nodded. "Yes, Mr. James," he whispered.

"Why on earth would you take frogs into Mr. Butler's gallery?" James asked in an even tone.

Taking a step forward, Percy placed his hands on the desk. "Timmy told me 'bout the art museum."

"It is a gallery, young man," Mr. Butler snapped. "A fine art gallery, not a museum."

"A gallery," Percy repeated with a firm nod as if he had meant that all along. "But I thought it were a museum like Montague 'ouse. They've dead animals there, you know, but I thought live ones'd be better for the people, so they can pet 'em and enjoy 'em, not jus' look at 'em." He turned to the gallery director. "I'm sorry if I made a mess of yer gatherin', Mr. Butler. I didn't mean nothin' by it. I jus' thought I'd help."

James dropped his head into his hands and groaned. Vicky placed her hands on the boy's shoulders once more and pulled him back to her. "Mr. Butler," she said, "I believe I understand Percy's actions today. If you will allow me to explain, I think it will shed some light on his actions."

"Very well," the man said, that scowl deepening if that were possible. "I must explain today's events to Mr. Easterling and pray I still have employment. My wife, Susanna, will never forgive me if I lose this position, and I fear her far more than I fear Mr. Easterling."

"I completely understand," Vicky replied. "You see, we recently took Percy to Montague House, and although he appreciated the art," she dug the tips of her fingers into his shoulder when the boy turned to argue, "but he was more interested in the collection of insects displayed in the science area."

Mr. Butler's expression changed and his eyes took on a far-off look. "I must admit I was inquisitive about such matters at his age. I spent hours looking through my father's books on insects from the Society of Aurelians. Such a tragedy when every member of that esteemed organization perished in a fire years ago…" He shook his head. "My apologies, Miss Parker, you were saying?"

"I have reasoned out," she continued, "that Percy believed your gallery was lacking…creatures." She stifled a shiver as images of Percy's 'friends' came to mind. "His actions were not done in malice but rather out of a sense of kindness. Percy believes that his affection for said creatures is shared by all, and although it may sound absurd, I can assure you he had no ill intentions with his actions at your place of business."

Mr. Butler pursed his lips. "I see."

"Percy has been with us for only a short time, and although he truly is a good boy, he is still learning. We spoke to him about not bringing spiders and frogs and whatnot home with him, but as your gallery is not a home, at least not in how he would see it, he may have assumed his bringing frogs inside fell outside of the rules set before him. He has not brought home any living creature since those rules were presented to him."

Percy nodded. "Charlie was me spider. He used to live in my bedroom, but Miss Vicky 'ad me return 'im to the park where 'e found a new 'ome so 'e wouldn't be away from 'is family."

Vicky glanced at James, who seemed as unsure as she as to how well Mr. Butler was taking this information. Gone was the man's scowl and in its place was a thoughtful expression. She wished she could hear what he was thinking.

Her wish was granted. "When I was a child Percy's age, I had a pet toad I named Henry." His voice had a hint of nostalgia to it. "I could not fathom why my mother threatened to whip me when I brought him to dinner one evening. Perhaps I have forgotten what it is like to be a young boy." He chuckled and looked at Percy. "I do have one question I would ask you, young man. How did you get past the doorman?"

Percy shrugged. "It were fairly easy, sir. He were talkin' to some lady, all smilin' at 'er like she were some sorta sweet, so 'e didn't pay me no mind. I didn't even 'ave to try 'n sneak in, I jus' up 'n walked right through the front door."

Mr. Butler heaved a heavy sigh and stood. "Perhaps today's events have shed some light on matters that must be addressed, specifically in the area of security. But please, young Percy, I ask that you not return to the gallery until you are much older. And without the company of anything that is not human."

James stood and walked around the desk. "I assure you he will not bother you again. And our sincerest apologies, sir. Please know that we will speak to Percy at length concerning his behavior."

Mr. Butler smiled and rested a hand on Percy's shoulder. "Go easy on the boy," he said. "I can now appreciate his actions quite well. Not condone, mind you, but I do understand."

As James walked the gallery director to the door, Percy turned around, removed the hat Vicky and James had gifted him for his birthday several months earlier, and looked up at Vicky. "Yer not gonna send me to the orph'nige, are ye?"

"The orphanage?" Vicky asked, taken aback. "Of course not. Why would you think such a thing?"

Percy shrugged. "Timmy says that's what's gonna 'appen to me." He shoved his hands into the pockets of his trousers and sighed. "'Ow much do ye think ye'll get fer me?"

Vicky wrapped her arms around him. "Percy, Mr. James and I like you too much to ever send you away. Nor would there be enough money in the entire world to get us to sell you." She lowered herself so she was face to face with him. "But we will talk about this matter of the art gallery later."

James returned and said, "All right, Percy, do you understand what you did wrong?"

The boy shook his head. "No. I was only tryin' to 'elp, is all. What's wrong with that?"

"Helping people is one of the greatest deeds one can do in life," James said. "But many times we must ask before we help. Some people may not see helping in the same way we do and that is why we ask beforehand – so there is no misunderstanding. Do you understand?"

Percy nodded. "It's like Miss Vicky's scarf. If I wanna use it to play pirates, I 'ave to ask first."

Vicky had to stifle a giggle as she recalled the day she returned home to find James and Percy acting out a battle. They had used her favorite bonnet and scarf – as well as a few potatoes and forks to represent the king's armies – as theatrical pieces. She had been quite angry with them for not asking permission first.

"I imagine he has learned his lesson," she said. "Now, if you promise that you will not do something like this again, I believe we will be able to trust you to make better decisions in the future."

"I promise," Percy said with a vigorous nod. "What do ye say, Mr. James? Do ye believe me? Can ye trust me?"

James rubbed his chin and frowned. Percy glanced at Vicky, his brows knitted.

"I suppose I can trust you again," James said finally, and Percy let out a heavy sigh in response. "Just remember, it is oftentimes better to ask permission beforehand, especially when it comes to insects and other creatures. Is that clear?"

"Yeah," Percy said, replacing the hat on his head. "That one lady screamed so loud, I don' think the frogs'd like it there anyways."

This time Vicky could not stop herself from laughing. Percy had a wonderful heart, so she was certain he would not make that mistake again. He was a bright boy, after all.

He hugged her and then turned to hug James. "And ye're me parents now, a mum and da who want me. I can't wait to tell Timmy that yer not gonna sell me to the orph'nige. He's gonna be so s'prised!"

"As long as you know that James and I care very much for you," Vicky said, fighting back tears. "Now, would you like to eat before you go out and play again? And do not forget, your reading lesson is at three sharp."

"I won't forget," Percy said. "An' I already ate the bread an' cheese I took with me, so I'm not hungry now." He rubbed his stomach to punctuate his point.

Percy had grown up on the streets, and for a long time he spent his days running errands to make money to help support him and his mother. Now he had time to play with his friends, although many shopkeepers continued to rely on him from time to time.

Vicky's first reaction when he was placed in her care had been to make every attempt to settle him down, to keep him from roaming the streets.

Now she saw how important it was to him that he be free, so with great reluctance she had agreed – within reason. After all, she wanted him to be safe. In the afternoons, she taught him to read, write, and do arithmetic, and once he had learned the basics, she hoped to hire a private tutor.

"Go along, then," she said. Once he was gone, she turned to James. "Frogs in an art gallery?" she asked, chuckling. "I cannot believe he did that."

James laughed. "One thing about Percy is that each day brings about something new. I think the years ahead will be a toll on both of us."

Vicky nodded. Although they had discussed the future rarely, she was certain that one day she and James would marry. Together they would raise Percy as their son and oldest brother to their other children that were sure to come. For now, however, she enjoyed the new feelings she and James shared and would focus on them.

When Percy returned – just as the bells tolled three – Vicky spent an hour working with him on his writing. At times he became frustrated – likely from sitting in one place for more than several minutes than from the work itself – but he always did his best and never gave up.

Once the dinner dishes had been washed and dried, Percy had gone to bed, and James had returned home, Vicky found herself thinking of a life married to James.

Rain pelted the window as she considered where they would live. The small rooms above the office would suffice for the time being, but if they were to have children beyond Percy, the same would be much too confined.

Although she adored Percy, she hoped to one day have a daughter, a child who preferred not to dig in the mud or hunt insects and frogs.

How fun it would be to dress a girl in lovely dresses and brush her hair until it shone.

Thunder rumbled and the windowpanes rattled in their frames. A carriage came to a stop in front of the office. Strange. Vicky was not expecting anyone and especially at such a late hour.

A cloaked figure emerged from the vehicle, hunched against the rain as he knocked on the door. When she opened it, the light illuminated a man dressed all in black with a familiar face inside the hood.

"Good evening, Miss Parker," Lord William Gerard said. "It is good to see you again." The baron had been a guest at Stanton Estate, the home of the Duke of Everton, several months earlier. She and James had been invited to a party, as was this man.

"What do you want?" Vicky asked without consideration for his title or station. Nor did she invite him inside. He had been rude at that party, arrogant, and went so far as to make veiled threats toward her in order to save his own skin.

"My sister has been murdered," the baron replied, "and I would like to solicit your help to find her killer."

Chapter Three

"My condolences for the loss of your sister," Vicky said as she poured the baron a cup of tea. She was uncertain why she had invited this man into her home, but perhaps it was because, like her father, she could not help but show kindness to all – even those who had wronged her in some way in the past.

"Mary Margaret was a spinster," Lord Gerard said. "I believe she will find better solace in death than she ever possessed in life. Our relationship was...spirited I suppose would be the best term to use. But that is over now that she is gone."

He spoke with such coldness, Vicky struggled to distinguish his tone from the drafts in the room. What she wanted was to get to the root of his request so she could get him to leave.

"My lord—"

He raised a hand to forestall her. "If you will be looking into the death of my sister, I see no reason for formalities. William, please. After all, once two people have met more than once, they become close friends, do they not?"

Vicky thought this the most ridiculous thing she had ever heard. If what he said were true, did that not mean that she should consider Mr. Clancy, the butcher, a close friend rather than the acquaintance he was and thus be using his Christian name? Or perhaps she should make the request of the baker, as well. She was certain the reserved Mr. Trumaine would not be as accommodating. Yet, if that was what the baron wished, she would do so. At least for the duration of this meeting.

Beyond that was far too much for her liking.

"Miss Vicky?" Percy stood in the doorway rubbing his eyes with the heel of his hand as he squinted into the room. "Are ye all right? 'E's not a thief, is 'e?"

Vicky hurried to the boy, placed a hand on his shoulder, and turned him about. "No, he is an acquaintance. Now, off to bed with you."

The baron arched an eyebrow. "I was unaware you had a child. I was under the impression you were unmarried." His tone expressed his assumptions quite clearly.

"He is not my son," Vicky replied as she returned to her place across the table from him. "He has been placed in my care. I suppose you can say I am his guardian. But I am sure you are not here to learn about who makes up my family. Now, concerning your sister's death—"

"Murder," he corrected. "Mary Margaret was found strangled in the graveyard of the church she attended. The constable believes the person used a rope to take her life. It is imperative I know who did this, and I trust no one, not even the constable, to find the information I so need. Which is why I have come to see you."

His matter-of-fact tone was somewhat unnerving. He may as well have been discussing the weather for all the remorse he exhibited. This was not the type of person of whom she could ever consider beyond an acquaintance. He had his place and she hers and that was how it had to remain.

She folded her hands in front of her. "My lord, we are not friends," she said in a crisp voice. "The last time we spoke, you had nothing but unkind words for me. More specifically, you made threats."

The baron heaved a great sigh. "And for that, I wish to apologize. I was under a great deal of pressure at the time, but I assure you, I did not mean a single word of it. Please, Miss Parker, I must have your help in this matter."

Vicky was uncertain whether or not his beseeching tone was genuine or simply a means to get her to do his bidding. "I cannot see how I could possibly be of any use in this matter, my lord. I am merely the daughter of an accountant. Surely you have connections with people far more suited to completing such a task."

"When you investigated the murder of the Duke of Everton," he said, "you were diligent in your inquest. I must say that I admired you for what you did, for what you learned. I have no doubt in your abilities to do the same in this case."

"I am not sure I agree," Vicky said with a shake of her head. "Finding a murderer is not an easy task. If it were, we would have no need for constables."

Lord Gerard leaned forward, his brown eyes glinting in the candlelight like an owl in the night. "Though I do wish to learn the identity of the man who took my sister's life, I am more concerned about what the murderer knows. I would like you to find him and learn the information I need."

"Information?" Vicky asked with a frown. "What sort of information?"

The baron leaned back in his chair but did not immediately respond. There was more to this story than he was revealing, Vicky was certain of it. Although she was genuinely sorry he had lost his sister, she was far too busy with work and Percy to play the sort of games of which the aristocracy was fond.

"I am sorry," she said as she stood. "I cannot help you."

"Eton School," Lord Gerard said. "Have you heard of it?"

"Of course. They have the reputation as the best boy's school in the country, quite costly and reserved for those willing to pay their exorbitant fees – although, I must admit those who do attend leave with an education that is unmatched by any other schools. Why do you ask?"

"What you say is true," the baron replied. "I attended Eton myself and feel that the education I received was well worth what my father paid. Every boy who has attended has become a great businessman, and I have no doubt the same would be for your boy. I have great influence with the headmaster there, and if I were to become his patron, I am certain they would accept him without hesitation. Aid me in this matter and when the boy is of age, I shall not only see he is accepted to the school, but I will pay his entire tuition, as well."

Vicky's head swam with various thoughts. Having Percy attend such a prestigious school would change his life forever. He would have access to an education and possible business connections that would do far more than any tutor she could possibly employ. An opportunity such as this would likely never be offered again.

Yet, she had her suspicions. "If I accept this offer, I must have your word you will see this agreement through. After all, the boy comes from a simple home. Why would they be willing to accept him, even with your endorsement?"

"Trust me, the headmaster will not refuse my request. You have my word. Find the information I need, and the boy will be given an opportunity he would otherwise never encounter. He will become a strong and successful man. Do we have a deal?"

Vicky had heard a story once about a woman who made a deal with the devil, and she was uncertain if this situation was any different. Was it worth a week or two of dealing with this man? Indeed, she believed it was, for by doing this task, Percy would have an entire world opened up to him that others like him would never encounter.

"Very well," she said, putting out her hand. "I agree, but you must keep back nothing. I must know everything, including this information you so need. In return, I promise I will do everything in my power to give you what you want. But keep in mind one important point; there is no guarantee that the information I gather is what you wish to know. And no matter what I learn, even if it leaves you with unanswered questions, you must keep your promise to see Percy is accepted into Eton School."

The baron shook her hand. "I always keep my word."

"Then tell me everything that will help me in this case," Vicky said, returning to her seat.

"Many years ago, our father fought for this country in the war against France. Upon his return, he spoke of a great treasure found there, which he brought back with him. How he managed to smuggle this gold and jewels into the country I do not know, but I do know he was never one to lie."

The baron lifted a finger and moved it back and forth across the flame of the candle that sat on the table between them, and his voice took on a distant tone. "Father did not drink often, but when he did, he would spend hours talking about how wonderful this treasure is. I begged him often to tell me its location, but he always refused. My mother tried time and again to get him to reveal it to her, but as they despised one another, she was less successful than I.

"The one person he did tell was Mary Margaret – on his deathbed. She had been a vibrant young lady making her debut into society, but after he spoke to her, she became a different person virtually overnight. And although she did not remove herself completely from society, whenever a possible suitor called, she looked upon him with suspicion and distrust."

He removed his finger from the candle and studied its tip. "Years passed and she became a spinster, though she never stopped allowing suitors to call. Strange, I know. It was not that she gave up on finding a husband. The way she explained it was that none were the perfect gentleman with whom she could trust with the knowledge of the treasure."

Vicky found the story intriguing. "Do you suspect that the one who took her life may have learned its location?"

Lord Gerard nodded and reached into the inside pocket of his coat. "I may not have stayed in contact with her as I should have once she went into hiding – or rather when she refused to see me – but I was able to gather some bits of information." He handed her a folded paper. "There are four men to whom you should speak. All had a romantic interest in my sister, and she them. These men dedicated the last few months of their lives attempting to woo her. I would like you to learn what they know concerning the location of the treasure."

Vicky took the piece of parchment and frowned. "You cannot truly believe they will reveal its location to the likes of me. Why would they?"

The baron chuckled. "Men tend to be braggarts, Miss Parker," he replied. "And they are more likely to brag in the presence of a beautiful woman. Excuse my forwardness, but I only speak the truth. I have no doubt that you will learn its location in no time."

The idea was absurd as far as Vicky was concerned. Unfolding the paper, she studied the names there and gasped. "Surely you do not believe a vicar was involved."

"And why not?" the baron asked. "He was counseling her, or so I was led to believe, but I know better. I saw how he gazed at her when she became of age. I believe he has had a romantic interest in her for years."

"And how would you know this if you have not been a part of her life?" Vicky asked.

"How I learned this does not matter," the baron said as he rose. "I would recommend beginning your inquiry with Reverend Lesson. He is the most likely to have what I need."

Vicky glanced at the list once more and frowned. "But the church is located in Edgeware. That is nearly ten miles outside of town. I have no way to get there."

Lord Gerard waved a dismissive hand at her. "I will send a carriage around for you tomorrow morning at ten." He reached into his coat pocket once more, this time producing several notes. "For any expenses you may incur."

Vicky had to swallow a gasp. It was one thing to see ten pounds written in a ledger but quite another to see it sitting on her kitchen table!

"How long do you estimate this will take?" he asked.

"I am unsure," Vicky replied. "I will begin with the vicar tomorrow and let the clues lead me the rest of the way. There simply is no telling without having spoken to any of these men."

"Very well," the baron replied. Vicky followed him to the front door. "The moment you learn of the location of the treasure, report to me immediately. I own the premises in which the tailor shop is located on Oxford Street. There you can leave a message with Mr. Rightford, the shop's proprietor. I am away on business too often and leaving word with my servants is not ideal. They gossip far too much for me to trust them with such important information no matter how much I threaten to sack them."

"I understand," Vicky replied.

As Lord Gerard stepped outside, he turned and glared down at her.

"Tell not a single soul about your findings concerning the treasure, Miss Parker. Many men would kill for such knowledge; in fact, they already have." Without waiting for a response, he pulled up his hood and hurried to the waiting carriage.

Vicky closed the door and locked it. What had she just agreed to? Was there truly a buried treasure located just outside of London? Before tonight, she would have dismissed such news as nothing more than foolish tales. Now, she was not so sure. If the baron knew of its existence, and his sister had been murdered because she held such knowledge, she had to assume that it did indeed exist. The question now was, would it still be where the late Lord Gerard had buried it?

The days ahead would be taxing, but the rewards would be far worth the trouble, for Percy would have the greatest opportunity any boy could have – a way to attend Eton School.

Chapter Four

James barked a laugh. "Buried treasure? That must be the most absurd tale I have ever heard."

It was just after nine in the morning, and Vicky had spent the good part of the past half-hour explaining Lord Gerard's call the previous evening. She was not all that surprised at his reaction, for had hers not been very much the same?

"Do you believe he is telling the truth?" James asked as he leaned against the larger desk.

"I do, or rather I believe Lord Gerard believes it. He said that his father returned from France after the war with a vast fortune and buried it, and although it resembles a story one might tell a child at bedtime, I believe he was told as much. Whether or not that treasure exists is another thing entirely." She walked up to James. "I hope you do not mind that I made the agreement to do this. I know I promised to speak to you before I made any big decisions, but how could I pass up such an opportunity for Percy?"

"Of course," James replied. "I likely would have done the same. Still, I am now caught between whether or not I believe the story to be true. It reminds me of similar tales men oftentimes share at the tavern when they have consumed too much drink. Take the story of the Earl of Pennington, for example."

Vicky crinkled her brow. "I do not believe I am familiar with that tale."

"The earl was known as a shrewd businessman, but he was also extremely distrustful of everyone around him, even his own children. He feared they would spend all he had earned, so he buried it and refused to reveal its location. As an old man, he began to lose his senses and became quite senile. On his deathbed, he called his sons together, for he had seen how they had grown into responsible men. His plan was to finally reveal where his wealth was hidden."

"How fascinating," Vicky said. "I presume his sons found it and therefore became wealthy."

James shook his head. "Sadly, by the time he died, he did not even recognize his own sons let alone the location of his fortune and was unable to recall where he had buried it. The estate eventually fell into bankruptcy, and even twenty years later, there are those still searching far and wide for the man's treasure."

The confidence Vicky had held before began to wane. What if she was unable to get any of the men to confess? What if it was someone other than one of those four men who had committed the murder and thus learned the information the baron requested?

As if hearing her thoughts, James smiled and said, "Do not worry. I have no doubt that you will find the information on this treasure. After all, you are Victoria Parker, and you can do anything you set your mind to."

An overwhelming warmth spread through Vicky, and it did not come from the sun shining through the window. It was strange how those in love could sense the worries of one another without speaking a single word aloud.

Before she could respond, Percy entered the room. "Buried treasure?" he asked excitedly. "I 'eard ye talkin' and I've 'eard the story 'bout the old baron an' 'is gold."

Vicky raised her brows. "Is that so? What did you hear exactly? I am interested in learning what you know."

Percy grinned. "The ole baron came back from France with so much gold, 'e couldn't fit it in jus' one carriage. See, he'd met this rich woman there, an' she were so rich, she owned ten 'ats!"

Vicky had to cover her mouth to keep back a giggle. His idea of rich was clearly far different from hers.

"She 'ad lots of 'orses an' dresses an' 'spensive jewelry, too. An' she gave it all to the baron so 'e could bring it here to bury in London." He sighed heavily. "Why'd anyone wanna bury a hat, I ask ye?"

"Who told you this story?" James asked.

"One 'a me mates 'eard it from 'is mum," Percy replied, "whose friend tole her." His eyes sparkled. "Are we gonna go out lookin' for it? I can dig if ye get me a spade."

Vicky laughed and walked over to remove his hat and ruffle his hair. "No, we are not going to search for it. You may go have fun with your friends. I will be returning late, so there will be no lessons today."

Percy gave what sounded suspiciously like a relieved sigh. "Good. I need a break. Me brain's needin' a good rest, it's been workin' so 'ard."

Vicky laughed again as she embraced him. "Now, off with you. But be sure to check in with Miss Laura at midday."

He stuck the hat on his head with a wide grin. "I will. Bye!" Then he bounded out the door.

With a look at the clock, Vicky decided she had time to complete some of her work before she was to leave, and soon, she and James were hunched over their desks.

Time passed much quicker than she realized, and before she knew it, James was standing behind her, saying, "The carriage has arrived."

She glanced up from her work. "Thank you." She returned the pen to its holder. "Will you see that this is returned to the bookshelf once the ink has dried? I should be back no later than four."

"Of course. And please be careful," James said as he walked her to the door. "I agree that the baron is harmless, but he is also very arrogant. Keep a watchful eye on everything around you and those to whom you speak, vicar or no. I do wish you would allow me to accompany you."

Vicky smiled up at him. "Do not be ridiculous. Someone must remain here to see to any clients who call. I will be safe, do not worry. And thank you for your concern. It is nice to know you care so much about my wellbeing."

Despite their confession of love for one another, his cheeks reddened. "If you believed I did not, you were clearly mistaken. Your wellbeing is always in the forefront of my thoughts."

"I will see you soon," she said, lifting herself onto the tips of her toes and kissing him.

Outside, the carriage driver stood at the door. "Miss Parker," he said with a bend at the waist, "Lord Gerard has instructed me to take you wherever you request. Where would you like to go first?"

"Are you familiar with the location of the church we must visit?"

"Very familiar, miss," he replied.

"Then that is where I would like to go."

He bowed again. "Very well, miss." He handed her into the carriage and closed the door, and soon they were moving down the street.

The traffic was heavy until they reached the outskirts of London, and soon the carriage was trundling past rolling hills at a quicker click. As she watched the passing cottages, she wondered about the people who lived there and the lives they must lead. What dreams did they have, and what stories did they tell?

So lost in her thoughts was Vicky that she was surprised when the carriage slowed and finally came to a stop. Had two hours already passed?

The driver opened the door and helped Vicky to alight from the vehicle.

To her left sat two identical thatch-roofed cottages with no more than a hundred feet between them. Both had black-trimmed windows and red doors and look quite inviting. To the right sat the church, a massive stone structure with stained glass depicting saints of long ago. Large trees and carefully manicured hedges surrounded the building, making for a peaceful setting.

Four stone steps led to a set of double doors that had been painted white, and Vicky took hold of the bronze handle and stepped inside. Her breath caught in her throat. Whereas from the outside the windows appeared plain, inside they lit up the nave with a bright blue glow. Red and gold carpets ran down the center aisle, and the wooden pews had been polished to a high sheen.

She walked through the building. No one seemed to be present, and she was afraid to call out and break the solemnity of the place. Then, through a door at the back, she heard someone singing. Stepping outside once more, she found a silver-haired man squatting down, a trowel in his hand and a bucket of mortar at his side.

"She was the finest beauty of all the land, with hair the color of wheat..." He rose and when he turned, he let out a yelp.

"Forgive me," Vicky said as the man clutched at his chest. "I did not mean to startle you. I suppose I should have made a bit more noise to announce my presence."

The older man chuckled. "You are just fine, miss. I lost a goodly amount of my hearing over the years, so I likely would not have heard you anyway. If I am not focusing all my attention when someone is speaking, I am unlikely to catch all he says." He motioned to where he had been working. "I often do the repairs during the week. The church is slowly falling into disrepair and is always in need of work. It is becoming more difficult with each passing year, but I do the best I can."

"Are you the caretaker?" Vicky asked.

The man set the trowel in the bucket and laughed. "Among other titles," he said, wiping his hands on a cloth. "But my main title is vicar." He put out a now-clean hand. "Reverend Henry Lesson."

Vicky felt her face heat. "My apologies," she said. "I assumed that with the work you were doing, you were not a member of the clergy."

He laughed. "I can see why you would come to that conclusion," he said, glancing at his stained clothing. "And who might you be?"

"I am Miss Victoria Parker. I do not mean to disturb your work, but I was hoping to speak to you if that is possible."

"Of course," he replied, his smile widening. "There is no finer counsel than that of a vicar. So, what is troubling you? These can be trying times in which we live. You made the right decision in deciding to share your burdens."

"I believe you misunderstand," Vicky said. "I am here to speak to you about the death of Mary Margaret Gerard."

The friendly smile disappeared, replaced with a scowl. The old vicar crossed his arms and narrowed his eyes. "Is this to grease the rumor wheel?" he demanded. "I refuse to have anything to do with gossip. It is a sin."

"Not at all," she assured him. "I am a friend of the family and was hoping to understand why anyone would want to take her life. Whatever you may know can help in my inquiry."

"Inquiry?" Reverend Lesson asked. "There was no inquiry into her death. Lord Gerard paid handsomely to silence the constable and keep him from doing any investigating. I understand that they devised some sort of story about a madman who escaped capture by running off to Scotland after murdering the poor woman."

Vicky stared at the vicar. "The baron bribed the constable?" she asked. "Why would he do such a thing?"

The vicar sighed. "Because Mary Margaret knew the location of the treasure, of course. Once she revealed it to her brother, he had her murdered so she could not claim any of it for herself. Follow me, Miss Parker, and I will tell you all you need to know."

Vicky followed after the man. "Concerning the baron?" she asked.

"Oh, yes," Reverend Lesson replied. "He, Mary Margaret, their father, and a feud that goes back many years. That would be the best place to begin, do you not think so?"

Chapter Five

Vicky stood beside the vicar, looking up at the church. It indeed was in need of repair, although she had not noticed that fact until Reverend Lesson had pointed it out. At least the front remained well-maintained.

"Many people have attended services here at this church, Miss Parker," the vicar said. "Many of whom were lost. That was the problem with the former Baron Cornelius Gerard and his wife, Lady Patricia Gerard, parents to William and Mary Margaret. The two argued incessantly – their marriage was one of convenience, you see, and each despised the other because of that arrangement. I do not say this as a means to gossip about them but rather to give you an understanding of why their offspring became who they are."

"Are you saying their dissatisfaction seeped into the lives of their children, making them unhappy, as well?"

"Indeed," Reverend Lesson replied as he strolled down a stone path that skirted the church building. "The Gerards attended church sporadically when the children were young but later came on a more regular basis. Or rather Cornelius brought the children more often, even going so far as to attend weekday services." He shook his head. "That is of little consequence now. There was a distinct rivalry between father and son, as there oftentimes can be. I overheard the two arguing over one matter or another quite often and eventually they simply stopped speaking to one another. Sadly, Cornelius died before they were able to reconcile."

He pointed ahead. "I will take you to the graveyard."

They walked through a wrought iron gate into the sacred area where row upon row of stone markers, some speckled with green or white moss, displayed the names of loved ones who had passed on. Trimmed rich emerald grass created paths between the stones and the tall thin trees that grew around the perimeter did little to shield the sun.

"Tell me about Mary Margaret," Vicky said. "Or at least what you knew of her."

"Mary Margaret was a rare beauty," the vicar said as he came to a stop before a particular headstone. "Any man who looked upon her was enamored by her. A sizable allowance from her father's estate gave her a life of luxury, which in turn gave her the perfect opportunity to become as vain as many of her kind do. Yet, she remained humble, dedicating her life to various charities."

Vicky looked upon the name engraved on the headstone, but it was unfamiliar. "Is this where Mary Margaret was found?"

Reverend Lesson nodded sadly. "It was just after sunrise. I had awakened thinking I heard someone cry out. By the time I arrived, Mary Margaret was already dead, a rope around her neck. One of the church lanterns lay there," he pointed to a stone beside the marker, "but I have no idea from where it came."

Vicky shivered at the image that appeared in her mind. "What do you think she was doing here at such an early hour? Would her driver not have heard her cry and come to her aid?"

"Her driver?" the vicar asked, confusion etched on his features. "I thought you knew. She lived here on the grounds."

"I beg your pardon?"

"Not here, exactly," Reverend Lesson said. "The land belonging to the church extends beyond the fence and includes the two cottages there." He pointed to the houses Vicky had noticed upon her arrival. "Three months ago, William requested that I allow his sister to stay here. For her protection."

"Did he happen to mention from whom or what she needed protection?"

The vicar nodded again. "From the men he arranged to call on her. You see, Mary Margaret decided of her own accord that she no longer wished to remain a spinster. It would be no easy task finding a man willing to marry her because of her age, but she wished to begin that journey, nonetheless. The baron offered to help by selecting three men of whom he approved, and she agreed to choose from them. Then each man called on her. What she did not know was that her brother had paid them to be her suitors."

Vicky recalled the list of names the baron had given her. "Do you not mean four? Lord Simon Faegan, Earl of Vantshire, Mr. Christopher Haring, Mr. Donald Galpin, and you."

The vicar's brows rose in surprise. "I was not asked to be her suitor, Miss Parker. I was asked to keep a watchful eye on Mary Margaret, which I did to the best of my ability. The other three were the men asked to call on her at the cottage in which she stayed. They typically stopped by in the afternoon, but late evenings were not unheard of. I did my best to make sure they maintained a level of decorum."

"And did you receive payment for your protection?"

"I refused initially, but the baron can be very persuasive when he wants to be and so I did accept his payment in the end. Do not think poorly of me, Miss Parker. I would have watched over her regardless." He looked out across the grounds, his eyes taking on a far-off look. "Mary Margaret confided in me that she knew her brother's motives were not pure, yet she played innocent to that knowledge." He sighed. "She confided much to me." His smile returned, and it was so wide, the corners nearly touched his ears. "We shared in meals and talked quite often. I suppose you can say that we became close."

Vicky did her best to organize the new information she had received, but one thing bothered her. "I was under the impression that Lord Gerard wanted nothing to do with his sister," she said as they resumed their stroll. "Are you saying that this was not the case?"

The vicar laughed. "William gave her everything she wanted, though she never made any requests. He spent a great deal of time trying to gain her confidence so she would tell him the location of a treasure revealed to her on their father's deathbed."

"Then the story is true?" Vicky asked, coming to a sudden stop. "Her father did indeed return from France with a great deal of gold and jewels?"

"The story is as true as the sky above is blue," the vicar replied. "Though their father never revealed to me where he had buried it, he did confess he had brought back a great treasure from France. I had inquired of Mary Margaret as to its location – not for my own gain but to protect her from those who would use her to get to it – yet she refused to tell me, and I did not press her. After all, what would a simple vicar do with such a treasure?" He sighed. "Who would have thought that someone would murder her despite my attempts to keep her safe?"

"I am sure you did what you could," Vicky said. "If I may ask, what happened during her stay? I assume she continued to allow the men to call on her despite knowing the truth about her brother paying them."

The vicar nodded. "She did. One day, one of the men would arrive and attempt to woo her. The following day, another would call. Sometimes, all three would call at different times throughout the afternoon and evening. I believe one of them caught her eye, for after a while, her demeanor changed. She spoke of trusting one, though she did not reveal who."

"Certainly you had an inkling which man she preferred, did you not?"

They came to a stop before the cottage closest to the church. "In all honesty, I cannot say, but I will say this. She came to love her brother in the end, for despite his willingness to give those men money, she believed she had somehow broken through his cold heart. But I am skeptical. It is unlikely that he reciprocated the feelings. You see, I have no doubt that she told him – her brother, that is – where to find the treasure, and once he learned that information, he murdered her."

Vicky stared at the vicar. "And what brings you to that conclusion?" she asked. "Was the baron here the morning you found his sister dead?"

"He was," Reverend Lesson replied.

"And the night of her death?"

"The baron was the first to arrive and the others came later." He frowned. "None left before sunset. I tried to tell her time and again that it was inappropriate for her to be alone with men to whom she was not married, but she refused to heed my warnings."

He opened the door to the cottage and stepped aside to allow Vicky to enter into a short corridor with two doors on the right, one on the left, and one at the back.

"Do you mind if I look around?" she asked.

"Not at all," the vicar replied. "I have work to see to, so if you do not mind being here alone, you can find me at the church once you are finished."

Vicky smiled. "Not at all, Reverend. And thank you."

He bowed and left through the front door, leaving Vicky alone in the entry corridor.

She went first to the door to the left, which opened to a sparsely-furnished sitting room with two chairs, a settee, and a table between them. A worn rug beneath the furniture was the only decorative piece in the room besides a simple cross that hung on the wall.

"For a woman who could afford luxury, Mary Margaret Gerard certainly did not live an extravagant life," Vicky mused.

On the settee lay a folded blanket and a pillow. The vicar had mentioned that the suitors would stay late on occasion. Surely she did not allow any of them to sleep overnight in her house. And why not offer him the second bedroom rather than the settee? Unless the second room was used for other purposes.

The first of the two doors to the right of the entry corridor hid away a bedroom, which contained a bed, a washstand, and a few pegs with dresses hanging from them along one wall. A variety of footwear lined the floorboard.

A piece of parchment caught Vicky's attention, and she went to the nightstand where it lay, unfolded it, and scanned its contents. It was addressed to someone named Sophia, and although the first paragraph was of little import – it spoke mostly of their long-lasting friendship – the second half was much more interesting.

Therefore, I wish to share with you my wonderful news. I have scheduled a time for each man who has confessed his undying loyalty to me to come tonight to share in a glass of wine and a bit of conversation. Three I shall send away, but to one I will reveal the treasure I mentioned to you in my last correspondence.

Vicky recognized the list of names given to her by Lord Gerard, but one more name caught her attention, and she returned the unfinished letter to the nightstand. "So, already someone has lied to me," she whispered aloud. "And you, Mary Margaret, you had planned to reveal the location of the treasure to one of your suitors, but who was the man you chose?"

Well, she would find no answers standing here and so she went to look through the remainder of the house.

The second bedroom was an exact copy of the first but it appeared to be unused.

The last door led to a kitchen with a small table and two wooden chairs. On the counter beside the sink sat a collection of wine glasses – five in total. A small amount of dried red liquid spotted the bottom of each.

What Vicky found more interesting, however, was the single glass that sat on the table. Why had it been left untouched?

Having seen enough, Vicky returned to the church. She once again found the vicar working on the stone wall as he had been upon her initial arrival, this time whistling as he worked.

"You were not completely honest with me, reverend," Vicky said, causing the man to start. "You did not seek to counsel Mary Margaret as you said but instead vied to earn her trust. Were you as interested in learning the location of the treasure as all the others?"

The vicar turned to face her. "That is preposterous! I am far too old to catch her eye."

"Yet you were invited to share in a glass of wine with her the night before her murder, were you not? Were you angry with her when she sent you away after your attempts to woo her had failed? Or did you become jealous when you learned she had chosen to reveal the truth to someone other than you?"

"My parishioners are poor!" Reverend Lesson cried. "I admit that in the beginning, I did hope she would reveal where the treasure was hidden so I could do the repairs needed on the church and to see that those who were in need had food and clothing. But as I came to know Mary Margaret as the woman she truly was – young, beautiful, and intelligent – I realized that the treasure was unimportant. I fell in love with her, Miss Parker, but when I professed my feelings for her, she did not believe me. Then she told me she would be leaving the following day…"

"How did you react to this news?" Vicky asked.

The sadness on the vicar's face deepened. "I shouted at her, but I regretted doing so as soon as I did. My temper can get the best of me at times…"

He took a step toward Vicky, and her heart began to pound in her chest. The illusion of the friendly vicar was gone, and she wondered if the man who replaced him was a murderer. His scowl did not help matters in the least.

"She had fallen in love with that fool of a drunk Donald Galpin and even allowed him to stay in her home despite my counsel that doing so would sully her reputation! I begged her to send him away, but she refused to heed my warning."

"How did you learn that he had stayed the entire night with her? And did she tell you that Mr. Galpin was the man she had chosen?"

"Well, no," the vicar replied. "But she did not need to. It was quite clear, for he spent more time than anyone else with her, and most nights he did not leave until after midnight. Sometimes it was not until much later." His face was a bright red. "There are words for women who allow men to stay late in their home, but I shall not speak them." He drew in a deep breath and then slowly released it. "After she asked me to leave that night, I returned to eat alone. I heard her other 'guests' arrive, for my kitchen window faces her cottage, and that only worsened my pain. I ended up drinking all of my wine."

"I see," Vicky said flatly. She had no pity for him. "What happened next?"

"I fell asleep in my chair and awoke when I heard her cry for help. I hurried outside, but as the sun had yet to rise, I stumbled as I made my way to the graveyard."

"Did you see anyone?"

The vicar shook his head. "No, but her brother told me the night before that once he learned the location of their father's treasure, Mary Margaret was as good as dead."

Chapter Six

Vicky sighed as she hung her hat on the peg in the vestibule of the office. The results of her visit to Edgeware were helpful to her inquiry, but she was glad to be home. A nice cup of tea and perhaps a short nap before dinner sounded wonderful. She wished she had slept in the carriage on her return journey but the jostling had not allowed her to do so. Thoughts of all she had learned during her visit had left her with too much to ponder – and an aching head.

"You must straighten your posture, James," a female voice Vicky did not recognize said from the other side of the door that led to the office. "Much better. Perfect posture leads to perfect results."

Who could that be? Vicky wondered as she opened the door.

James stood beside the bookcase that held their clients' ledgers. At the larger desk sat an older woman with graying hair pulled back into a severe bun at the nape of her neck. Emeralds hung from her ears, matching those on her necklace.

"Hello, James," Vicky said as she pulled on the fingers of her gloves to remove them. "Who do we have here?"

He jumped at her voice. "Oh, Vicky, I have the most wonderful news. This is my aunt Miriam Watson. She is visiting London for the next few weeks and has stopped by to see me."

"It is a pleasure to finally meet you, Mrs. Watson," Vicky said.

"James has told me much about you."

The truth was that James had shared little about the woman who had raised him upon the death of his parents, who had perished in a carriage accident when he was ten. Vicky had assumed his reluctance to speak of her stemmed from the fact he preferred not to discuss his parents' death, which was understandable, and she never pressed him about it. His story would come to light when he was ready. Regardless, Vicky was pleased to finally meet such an important member of his family and would do what she could to make his aunt feel welcome.

She walked around the desk. "There is no need for such formalities. Miriam will do just fine." A tall, formidable woman, she did not bend her neck to study Vicky. Instead, she looked down her nose as if she were inspecting a horse's stall that had yet to be mucked out.

"James tells me you are his employer," Miriam said. "Is this true?"

Good, she was straightforward. "It is," Vicky replied.

"And were you trained in accounting?"

"I was."

The older woman's brows raised in surprise. "Formally? Certainly there are no schools that accept women accountants."

Was this how suspects in an inquest felt when Vicky questioned them? She certainly hoped not. "My father started the firm many years ago, thus the name Parker Accounting. I spent a great deal of my younger years watching him work and he eventually trained me. When he passed away, I took his place." She turned and smiled at James. "Your nephew has been a tremendous help, oftentimes doing far more than what is asked of him. I would not be as successful without him."

"All women need a man in their life if they wish to succeed," Miriam said, her lips in a sly smile only Vicky could see. "Men have a head for business where women do not, and my darling nephew is no exception. Tell me, have you signed over the firm to him yet? Or will you wait for it to happen naturally once you are married? If you do marry, of course." The twist of her mouth tightened into disgust before she waved a dismissive hand. "Perhaps it is for the best, really.

James is a very eligible bachelor with a great deal of ability, and he will need a woman willing to set aside her interests to help him reach his greatest potential."

For a moment, Vicky could only stare in stunned silence. She had seen that look on many women during her lifetime, and the meaning had always been the same – condescension.

So, she does not approve, Vicky mused. Or was it that she only approved if Vicky learned her place? It would not be the first time someone had opposed her position at the firm and it likely would not be the last. That did not mean she had to accept being treated as less than she was.

The truth was, she and James had agreed to keep their romance private for the time being, but did he not have every right to tell the woman who raised him about the possibility of marriage? Of course he did. What Vicky did not appreciate was his aunt deciding who should take control of Parker Accounting. Their current arrangement was working just fine, thank you very much, and no one would dictate to her that anything needed to change, marriage or no marriage!

"We have yet to discuss what path our future will take," Vicky said, doing her best to control the annoyance in her voice. "But when we come to a decision concerning our lives outside of our business arrangement, we will be sure to inform you. Otherwise, I see no reason to discuss Parker Accounting with you or anyone else outside of the firm."

Miriam gasped and pressed a hand to her breast. "I have never felt so attacked in all my life," she cried.

Vicky grasped her skirts to keep from rubbing her temples. It was just as she suspected; this woman was an actress without a stage!

"I merely asked a simple question," Miriam continued, "yet you make it seem as if I am asking about every intimate detail of your relationship." She turned to James. "Will you not come to my defense as she humiliates me? No, of course not. I imagine it brings you pleasure seeing her attack me so."

"Not at all, Aunt Miriam," James said, hurrying over to take her by the arm. "Vicky did not mean any offense, I can assure you.

She simply meant that we wish to discuss things before we speak to others about our plans."

Seeming to be appeased by this response, Miriam waved away James. "I am pleased to hear this, but does Victoria feel the same?" Her eyes bore into Vicky's.

Crafty old hag, Vicky thought.

Then she paused. Where had such a hateful thought come from? Perhaps her immediate reaction had forced her to misjudge Miriam. After all, his aunt had been an important part of James's life and would only want what was best for him.

Plus, the beseeching look James gave made her rethink her response. Perhaps Miriam deserved the benefit of the doubt.

"It is only right that James confides in you," Vicky said aloud. "But as to marriage, we have not yet broached the subject."

James's gaze dropped humbly as he addressed his aunt. "What Vicky says is true. We have not yet discussed marriage. And although it is what I want, I will not ask for her hand until she is ready."

Miriam frowned. "Why do you call her by that name?" she asked, her brow knitted in displeasure. "Her name is Victoria. Would it not be more appropriate to address her as such? The other is so…common." She said the last as if it left a bitter taste on her tongue.

James shook his head and smiled. "Oh, no, Aunt Miriam. It is a privilege to call her Vicky. That name is reserved for those closest to her. She has extended that invitation to only a few, and they consider it an honor when offered."

His aunt snorted as she ran a hand over the desk beside her. "Well, I cannot stop you from doing so," she said offhandedly. "But you should know that there was a woman in the village where I was raised who went by that name. She was known for a certain type of…employment…that a decent woman would never discuss in public. Therefore, I would prefer to address her as Victoria. After all, that is her Christian name."

When she looked at James, she nearly pouted! "Perhaps the instruction I gave you has failed. Or is it that you are no longer finding my advice meritorious?"

Vicky retracted her previous thoughts about giving this woman the benefit of the doubt. She had been in her presence only five minutes and already disliked her. What surprised her the most was how quickly James submitted. "No, Aunt Miriam, I will address her as Victoria when we are in your presence if that pleases you."

Miriam patted his cheek as if he were still a young boy. "You have such a good heart, James, just like your father. I knew you would never hurt me for the sake of a woman."

If Vicky did not leave soon, she was concerned her glower would send his aunt bursting into flame.

No! she thought. *This is my office and therefore I have every right to be here.*

Rather than being the object of disapproval, perhaps it was best if she sat and worked until she and James were alone, otherwise she might say something she would later regret.

"It has been a pleasure meeting you," she said, doing her best to make her smile as warm as possible. "However, I have some work I must attend to. If you will excuse me?" She did not wait for Miriam to respond but instead went straight to her desk and sat.

"You were not lying?" the older woman sputtered. "She truly does work?" She pursed her lips for a moment. "I see now what has transpired here. It is as clear as mid-afternoon."

Vicky ignored her, but James asked, "What do you mean?"

"It is improper for an unmarried woman to be in such close quarters with a man alone," his aunt replied with a whisper that carried through the room. "Untrained women will often put themselves into positions where they can tempt the men around them. I find it remarkable that you were able to complete any work at all!"

Vicky slammed closed the ledger before her and stood so quickly, her head spun. "I can assure you—"

"That it was I who approached Vicky," James interrupted. "Or rather Victoria. You will not meet a woman more professional. She is brilliant and well-mannered and possesses a sterling reputation."

"Be that as it may," Miriam said, "it is still improper. However, if James insists that there has not been any…misbehavior, then I believe him."

"And I can assure you that he speaks the truth," Vicky said.

Miriam rolled her eyes, and Vicky considered putting her in her place. But no, Miriam had taken in James when he had no one and thus deserved respect, even if she was unwilling to return it. Biting her tongue would be painful but it would lead to a much more pleasant visit for everyone.

"I must admit," Miriam said, her demeanor now pleasant, "I am jealous of what you are capable of doing. If I spoke harshly, it is only out of concern for my nephew. I simply want what is best for both of you. I hope you understand that."

It was not an outright apology, but it was likely the closest Miriam would come. "Thank you," Vicky said.

To Vicky's surprise, Miriam hugged her, leaving her speechless.

"Now," Miriam said once the embrace ended, "we must go shopping soon to buy you some new dresses. A lady should wear fine fabrics, not this course near-burlap you wear." She turned and walked toward the vestibule. "I will come by tomorrow to discuss our plans while I am here."

Vicky offered a quick "Good day" but found she could not move. James accompanied his aunt to the front door and returned a few minutes later.

"You must understand," he said with a laugh as he closed the door between the vestibule and the office, "she means well but her opinions are oftentimes misconstrued."

"Her opinions are one thing," Vicky said. "What I would like you to explain is why you mentioned marriage to her before we have even broached the subject."

James sighed. "I realize I should not have spoken out of turn, but when I was bragging to her about how brilliant you are, the words came of their own accord. I am sorry."

Vicky hugged him. He could have said worse about her, she supposed. "It is all right, but please remember, this decision about marriage is for us to make. I do hope to be engaged before she begins planning our wedding."

He smiled down at her. "I promise that I will not mention it again. For now." He walked over and dropped into his chair. "Now, tell me what you learned today during your outing."

Chapter Seven

The following morning, Vicky prepared a breakfast of eggs and liver and watched with curiosity as the boys ate. James was not present for the earlier meal on most days, eating at home rather than here, but when he did come for breakfast, he and Percy could make quite a spectacle of themselves. Indeed, those of the male persuasion tended to forget all basic table manners whenever it suited them.

Percy had grasped a knife in one hand and a fork in the other and was stabbing bits of eggs like some sort of warrior before each bite. Rather than correcting him, James was telling him a story about an incident that happened while he was at school – in between shoveling food into his mouth as if it might disappear from his plate at any moment. Vicky could not help but wonder if this was how men ate before training in manners became popular.

"It was then when the master stared down at me," James was saying before he deepened his tone, "'Kensington, did you fall asleep?'"

Percy stopped to stare at him, fork halfway to his mouth and his eyes wide. "What did ye tell 'im?"

"I could not tell him that I had indeed fallen asleep or I would have been sent to the headmaster's office, and trust me, you do not want to be sent there under any circumstances! No, I told him I was merely allowing my eyelids to rest."

Percy dropped his fork with a loud *clink* on his plate and giggled.

"Then what? Did ye get inta trouble?"

James gave a sad nod and placed his hand on the table. "Do you see my missing fingers? The headmaster took them as my punishment."

Vicky stifled a laugh, but Percy frowned and gave James a sidelong look. "I thought ye said a dog bit 'em off." His voice dripped with suspicion.

James nodded again. "It was the headmaster's dog. And it was the headmaster who commanded the beast to take my fingers! You should see the boy with the missing leg!"

This sent Percy into fits of laughter that had him doubled over at the waist.

Vicky sighed. "I was under the impression that I was minding one boy, not two," she said as she rose to collect the dishes. "Percy, go on and play with your friends, but do not forget, you are to check in by eleven today, not midday."

Percy nearly sent the chair flying as he leaped from it. "I won't ferget, Miss Vicky. I promise." He grabbed his hat and clapped it on his head before turning to leave.

"Excuse me," Vicky said with mock severity. "Are you forgetting something?"

The boy's eyes grew quite round. "Oh, sorry, Miss Vicky!" he said, hurrying over to throw his arms around her. "See ye later."

Vicky laughed as he hurried from the kitchen, and soon the front door banged shut. As Vicky continued clearing the table, James rose to help.

"It will be wonderful having Aunt Miriam spend time with us," he said. "She really is a lovely woman." He glanced toward the office. "It was unfortunate she was unable to meet Percy yesterday."

Vicky cringed at the thought of being forced to spend any amount of time with Miriam, but if she and James were to even consider marriage, what choice did she have? "Why have you not spoken about her more?" she asked. "Did the two of you have some sort of argument?"

James laughed. "Who would want to argue with her?"

Vicky could think of a dozen reasons one might have disagreements with a woman as cantankerous as Miriam seemed to be.

"I suppose it has something to do with the memories of my time with her. Or rather the fact that she was there when my parents were not. She is Mother's sister, and they looked so much alike. I do not like to be reminded of…" His words trailed off.

Vicky took his hand in hers. "I understand," she said. "I know the pain you endure."

Although her mother had passed away when Vicky was barely old enough to walk, she understood all too well the heartache of losing a parent. At least her father had been with her.

"I am sure you will do all you can to make certain your aunt's stay in London is comfortable."

James smiled. "You are as kind as you are beautiful," he said. Then, to Vicky's surprise, he gave her a small kiss. "We are not in the office, so we are breaking no rules," he whispered in her ear.

Vicky giggled. "You are a clever man, Mr. Kensington," she said. "However, we cannot spend our day dawdling. We have work to do."

"Is that what you call this, Miss Parker?" he asked with a wide grin.

She pushed him away with a playful shove. "You are far too brazen for your own good, Mr. Kensington," she said as she walked into the office.

Once at her desk, she opened the ledger she had not completed the previous evening, but she soon found her thoughts drifting to what she had learned about the murder the day before. Although the vicar had been truthful with some points, he had also lied about others. Also, the fact that Lord Gerard had paid her suspects to court his sister – who offered a man money to do such a thing, let alone three! – only complicated matters.

Tomorrow, she would speak to Lord Faegan. The address Lord Gerard had provided said he was located not fifteen minutes away by foot. It was certainly better than two hours by carriage!

Reaching for her pen, Vicky glanced out the window and paused at seeing the most curious sight. Andrew Thompson, the man to whom she had offered the new position, was marching down the footpath. In one hand he carried a bouquet of yellow flowers and a bottle of what appeared to be wine in the other.

"James," Vicky said, standing, "Mr. Thompson is…" A knock at the door halted her words.

She followed James to the vestibule and he opened the front door. There stood Mr. Thompson, a broad smile on his face.

"Miss Parker, Mr. Kensington." For a moment, he stood staring at them, much like a rabbit aware of a dog nearby. Then he thrust the items toward them. "A small gift of thanks for trusting me and allowing me to accept my new position in your firm." He said the words as if reciting them from memory.

"This is very kind of you, Mr. Thompson," Vicky said, "but there is no need for gifts. Would you not prefer to give them to Mrs. Thompson?"

The man shook his head. "It was her idea that I present them to you," he said. Then he sighed. "And now I feel foolish seeing as you do not want them."

James took the wine from him. "I, for one, will make good use of this." He lifted the bottle to punctuate his point.

Vicky took the flowers. "It is a very thoughtful gesture," she said, smiling, "and you may tell your wife that I said so." She glanced past Mr. Thompson. "Is Mrs. Thompson with you?"

"Oh, no. Jenny is with a friend, Molly Ellis, until the late afternoon." A frown appeared on his lips. "Which gives me reason for great concern."

"Do you feel her friend will influence your wife in a negative way?" James asked.

Mr. Thompson gave a sad nod. "I am afraid so, Mr. Kensington. "Molly has a significant interest in poetry…and no, that is not what worries me. Most women enjoy poetry. Molly, however, has convinced her husband to read it, as well. Not only does he read it, but he also recites it aloud to her! If Jenny came to me wishing that I recite poetry and news of this made its way through London, I will never be able to leave my house again!"

Vicky had to turn away to hide her smile.

Thankfully, James was able to keep his demeanor and placed a hand on the man's shoulder. "I believe you will be fine," he said. "There are far worse ways to embarrass oneself than enjoying a few lines of prose. Perhaps you can also memorize a description from a battle guide or something from Samuel Johnson or James Bruce to balance your learning."

Mr. Thompson released a relieved sigh. "Thank you, sir. That is a brilliant idea." He glanced around. "Since I am here, do you maybe have some work for me to complete today? I am willing to begin early if you would like."

"Come inside," Vicky said as she stepped back, leaving the door open to allow the cool breeze to blow through.

Mr. Thompson looked around expectantly, but his hands gripped his cap so tightly his fingertips turned white. It was clear he wished to make a good impression, yet he already had as far as Vicky was concerned. She gave James a tiny nod.

"I will return to work," James said. He lifted the bottle and added, "Thank you again for this."

Once James was gone, Vicky returned her attention to Mr. Thompson. "We agreed to offer you a position because you convinced us that you are a capable man, and we were impressed by you. The flowers are lovely and I will display them proudly. And although I will accept your gifts today, there is no need to bring something every time you are here."

"Yes, Miss Parker."

"Now, as to you working today, I do have an assignment for you if you are willing to accept it."

He gave an excited nod. "Oh, yes, please. Whatever you request, I will do."

"Enjoy this day – and the weekend – knowing that your position here is secure. Come Monday, report first thing in the morning ready to begin."

Mr. Thompson let out a sigh. "Very well," he replied. "And you are right. I tend to worry far too much. Jenny says I talk too much, and although I consider myself a quiet man, she is not the first person to describe me so. I think most who say so are only jesting, just so they can point out that I must speak more. People can certainly be judgmental. I remember a cousin—"

Fearing he would continue for the rest of the day, Vicky interrupted him. "Thank you again for the flowers. They are very beautiful. I probably should put them in water before they wilt."

A gasp made Vicky start, and she turned to see James's Aunt Miriam standing in the doorway, her mouth hanging open.

Oblivious to what had just occurred, Mr. Thompson said a quick "Good day to you", gave Miriam a nod of greeting, and slid past her and out the door.

"Please tell me that I did not see what I believe I saw," Miriam said, her lips twisted into a scowl. "Did you just accept flowers from that man? Who is he? And where is James?"

"Aunt Miriam?" James called from the office. He appeared in the doorway. "Well, hello. I did not expect you this early." He leaned in to kiss her cheek.

"You know I like to begin my day much earlier than most," she said. "James," she said his name slowly, "a man just gave Victoria flowers. Surely you do not find that acceptable."

Vicky's jaw ached with how tightly she clenched it. Did Miriam disapprove so greatly of Vicky that she would do whatever possible to keep James from being with her?

James simply laughed. "Oh, Aunt Miriam, that is Mr. Thompson, the new accountant we hired. He was merely giving her a token of thanks for being chosen for the position. He even gave me a bottle of wine." He paused to frown. "Surely you did not suspect anything improper was taking place?"

"Trust me," Vicky said, doing her best to keep her tone even, "she all but stated as much."

Miriam pursed her lips. "My dear," she said in an overly-sweet voice, "it was not about you I was concerned but rather that man. Women are easily manipulated with small gestures such as flowers. Forgive me for worrying about you. I assure you I meant no harm."

James smiled at Vicky. "You see? Aunt Miriam does care about you. I can see it in her eyes."

All Vicky could see in Miriam's eyes were judgment and condemnation, yet she reminded herself how important this woman was to James. "Would you like a cup of tea?" she asked, hoping the invitation would smooth over the animosity that had developed between them.

"I would love to," Miriam said, "but I have a busy day today. Do not worry about our plans, though, for I have created a schedule for all of us."

She removed a folded piece of parchment from her reticule and handed it to Vicky. "As you can see, I have scheduled several activities, including dinner at the Royal Mayfair, shopping on Regency Street, and an afternoon tea where I plan to introduce you to my friends."

Vicky glanced at the flowery writing that made up the list, which included places and times. "This is very kind of you," she said slowly, "and very well-thought-out, but I have responsibilities here that I cannot skirt." When Miriam frowned, Vicky quickly added, "But I see no reason we cannot choose one of these activities to do together." In truth, she would rather have cut off a toe than spend any amount of time with this woman.

Miriam gave her a look that reminded Vicky of a mother instructing a daughter. "Victoria, you should be spending your days enjoying life, not cooped up here all day. Once you and my nephew are married, you can finally forgo this pretense of working and take care of him and your home."

Before Vicky could respond, James said, "I can assure you, Aunt Miriam, that Vicky…erm…Victoria's position is not in pretense. Her mind is sharp and she could rank well with the best of men."

Pride filled Vicky, not only for his praise of her abilities but also that he had come to her defense.

That was quickly washed away when he added, "There is no need to worry. I will speak to her later concerning work."

"See that you do, my dear," Miriam said crisply. "Now, if you look carefully, you will see that I noted when you and I can spend some time alone on Sunday." She kissed James on the cheek. "And you, I will see later." With that, she turned and walked out the door.

With her temper threatening to boil over, Vicky turned to James. "Unless you have forgotten," she said, "this is my place of business. I will not have my schedule, nor my future, dictated by your aunt regardless of whether her intentions are well-meaning or not."

"I know," James replied, taking her hands in his. "And you have every right to be annoyed. Just remember that I agree only to appease her. My aunt is very opinionated, as I am sure you have noticed;

I am not blind to that fact. But she is only in London for a fortnight, and I doubt I will see her again for several years. I just ask that you tolerate her assertiveness for my sake."

He kissed her hands and her anger dissipated. James always sacrificed so much for her, and what he asked of her now was nothing compared to what he had done for her thus far. Her response, however, was not based on any sense of give-and-take but rather on what she wanted for him. "I agree to this only because of my love for you."

"And that is why I love you," he said, pulling her into his arms. "You are always willing to help me without complaint."

Although Miriam had stoked the anger inside her, Vicky was willing to endure the woman's intrusion into her life for James's sake. And the more she considered it, two weeks was not a long time. Surely she could get through it unscathed and the entire ordeal would be over with.

Chapter Eight

On Saturday, and with the office officially closed for the day, Vicky made her way down the footpath on Wellington Street. James had been more than willing to mind Percy, and she prayed the two would not burn down the house before she returned home. They were adorable but could be worse than ten children when they were together!

As Vicky walked past the many shops, returning smiles and greetings of the many proprietors with whom she was acquainted, her thoughts soon turned to Miriam. She would occupy much of their time over the next two weeks, but if Vicky made the effort to befriend James's aunt, perhaps it would make the woman's presence more bearable.

Today, she had to focus her attention on the murder of Mary Margaret Gerard and her next interview would be Lord Simon Faegan, Earl of Vantshire. The walk to his home would have taken less time if she had been willing to pass through The Mint, but Vicky would rather have walked an entire week than to return to that contemptible area. Known for housing thieves and prostitutes, Vicky should never have had reason to go there, and if it were up to her, she never would again.

Where she was going today was nowhere nearly as bad, but it was certainly not what she would have expected for a man of Lord Faegan's standing. The houses on Bowman Street consisted of small gardens and freshly painted facades, yet they seemed more appropriate for less prestigious families. Perhaps the earl had a mistress he kept there.

This section of the street sat on a steep incline, and a dog yapped as it barreled past her. A moment later, a young girl chased after it, giggling, a mop of blond curls flowing behind her. Vicky smiled, remembering when she had lived such a carefree life.

She stopped before number fifteen and glanced at the list Lord Gerard had given her. A man stood on the portico, one hand on his thigh and the other balled into a fist, threatening the gentleman at the door.

"Earl or not makes no difference, do you hear me?" the man bellowed. "You owe me money, and I demand payment! Either that or return that coat and I will find another man willing to pay for it!"

The earl smiled as he reached out and placed a hand on the man's shoulder. "Samuel," he said in a soothing tone, "my father purchased all his clothing from you, as do I. This is certainly not the way to treat your loyal patrons, now is it?"

"But your father paid his debts," Samuel replied. "He didn't gamble away all his money as you do. Now, I insist you pay me!"

Vicky stared in disbelief. Never had she heard of a tailor, or any proprietor for that matter, going to a client's home and demanding payment. And in such a public manner. And especially when it included a member of the *ton*.

"I will have your money by Monday," the earl replied, undaunted. "Now, I suggest you leave before I lose my temper."

"Monday?" Samuel said with a snort. "I want what's owed me now or I'll make sure everyone's aware of the untrustworthy lout you are."

The earl grabbed the man by his shirt and pulled him close. "Make no mistake, Samuel, I will burn down your shop myself if you raise your voice to me like this again. Do I make myself clear?"

A cold draft washed over Vicky when the tailor swore under his breath and hurried past her, nearly knocking her over in his rush. This was certainly not what she had expected to find upon her arrival to the home of an earl!

"My apologies, miss, for you being forced to witness such uncouth behavior," the gentleman said with a bow. "Dear Samuel has grown quite senile in his old age. You may move along without fear that he will harm you in some way."

"Are you Lord Faegan?" she asked.

The man raised a single eyebrow. "I am. Do I know you?"

Vicky shook her head. "I am Victoria Parker. I was a friend of Miss Mary Margaret Gerard."

For a moment, Vicky wondered if the man would respond, but then he heaved a melancholy sigh and said, "My beloved Mary Margaret. When I heard she had been murdered, I wept for the entire day." The tiny smile that played at the corner of his lips belied the sadness to his words. As did his overt assessment of Vicky. "If you are in need of a shoulder on which to cry, I am prepared to offer mine. I have been told that I am a wonderful listener."

"I appreciate the offer," Vicky said, curtailing the scowl that tried to twist her lips, "but I was hoping to ask you a few questions concerning your relationship with Miss Gerard and perhaps discuss the night of her death."

He looked past her and then over his shoulder. "There are some in London who hoped to learn what Mary Margaret knew and would do anything to gain that knowledge. Perhaps it would be best if you come inside so we can discuss it further."

What had she been thinking calling on a man without benefit of an escort? Perhaps she should have asked James to accompany her. Well, it was too late for regrets, and she had questions that needed answering.

Vicky followed Lord Faegan through a small entryway and into a sitting room. The furniture was covered in faded green fabric and the wood had more than a few nicks from age and wear. There were few decorative items, which surprised her. Should an earl not have the best in life?

"My staff is away for the weekend," the earl said with a small laugh as he led her to the sofa. "Sit, please. I am afraid I cannot offer you any tea. Perhaps you would like a glass of wine?"

"No, thank you," Vicky replied. The cushions were lumpy and uneven, threatening to spill her off the side. She glanced around the sparse room once more. "Forgive me for asking, but is this your main residence?"

"Indeed it is," he replied. "For the time being, that is. My country estate is under extensive renovation, and sadly, my home on Grosvenor Square is also receiving some much-needed repairs. This house is small, but it does suit my needs. I have a pillow on which to rest my head and food in the larder when I am hungry." He lifted his glass of brandy. "And I never run out of drink."

"I see. Well, I spoke to Reverend Lesson. He said that on the night of Miss Gerard's death, she had a number of men call over. I believe you were one of them, were you not?"

The earl snorted. "You make it sound as if she were some sort of harlot. But I am not surprised that old vicar painted such a picture of her. He was jealous of any man who called on her because he lusted after her more than any of her other suitors. It was quite pathetic if you ask me."

And yet I did not ask, she thought, making a mental note about how quickly he was willing to put a poor light on the vicar. Aloud, she said, "Is that so? Was he that forward?"

"As forward as a dog salivating over a bone," Lord Faegan replied, his mouth twisted in disgust. "He would do anything to be close to her, made every excuse to hold her hand or touch her arm. He is a disgrace to the clergy if you ask me."

Again, I did not, she thought, amused. "Yet Miss Gerard continued to speak with him?"

The earl nodded. "Mary Margaret was a kind woman, wise and beautiful. She could not bring herself to break the old man's heart. If I am honest, which I make every attempt to be, I believe she genuinely liked him, but then again, she liked everyone." He barked a laugh. "The men vying for her attention could never match me, though. I do not say so out of pure arrogance but rather because I am a handsome man. And I doubt there is any in the region who can match my wit if you ask me."

Vicky stifled a snort. "I understand that several men had been hired—"

"By Mary Margaret's brother?" Lord Faegan asked. "Indeed, and I was one of them. We were each tasked to woo her so as to learn the location of some treasure that their father had buried – or some such nonsense. I found the money I received…welcomed, but it was the spoils of the treasure itself that I looked forward to receiving."

A thoughtful smile crossed his lips. "Treasure." He repeated the words several times and then shook his head. "Gerard has been after that treasure for years. He became obsessed with learning its location when he was a young man, even going so far as to follow his father every time he left the house in hopes that he would be led to it. But Lord Gerard, the elder, was far too skilled at the art of manipulation, and the son lacked the ability to track him." He chuckled. "He would have been better off bringing in one of those buckskinned trackers from the Americas, for he had no idea what he was doing if you ask me."

"And did you ever learn the location of the treasure?"

"I?" he snapped. Then he closed his eyes for a moment. "Forgive me. Gerard has asked me that very question every day since Mary Margaret's death, and I will tell you what I told him. No, I did not."

"I see. Did you call on Miss Gerard the evening before she was found dead?"

He nodded. "I did."

"Would you tell me what transpired during your time there?"

The earl leaned forward and placed his forearms on his knees. "I called on her several times a week. We spoke of poetry, life in London, all of life's affairs. That last time was different, however, for Mary Margaret had written to me that she would be revealing the location of the treasure that night. I admit I was excited to learn this, but something happened during those frequent calls to her home. I came to respect her. She carried a heavy burden, one that no woman should be forced to carry, and I came to care for her more than the promise of riches."

He heaved a heavy sigh as he rose to refill his glass. "Are you sure you do not want a drink?"

"No, thank you," Vicky replied. "Please, go on."

Lord Faegan returned and dropped into his seat once more. "Despite my increased interest in Mary Margaret, I was unfortunately not the man with whom she chose to share her information. I remember that night quite well. I arrived just after ten, the moon casting its wondrous glow over the graveyard next door."

He frowned. "Well, there was a bit of fog, now that I think about it...Regardless, it was quite peaceful, and Mary Margaret greeted me with an embrace, as she often did. She invited me inside and poured me a glass of wine. Then we spoke of the day's events, and she ended the conversation by revealing that she would not be sharing the location of the treasure with me."

"And what did you do when she refused to share that information with you?"

The earl shrugged. "I told her that I understood and I wished her well. I do wonder who she did tell. I asked her, of course, but she refused to reveal it to me. Then that drunken vicar had to go and spoil a perfectly good evening."

Vicky raised her brows. "How so?"

"He tripped over something just outside the window. I went out and accused him of spying, but he took off into the shadows of a small work shed at the back of the property. I left soon after that. When I learned of Mary Margaret's death, I wished I had remained. In fact, there are many things I would have done differently."

The room fell quiet as Vicky consider this new piece of information. "Do you recall seeing anyone else – besides your encounter with the vicar, of course."

Lord Faegan took a long drink from his glass, and to Vicky's surprise, he wiped his mouth on his sleeve. "I did hear Gerard speaking with someone inside the old vicar's cottage. The window was open, and I recognized his voice, but I could not make out what they were saying." Then his eyes lit up. "I did see something interesting when I left."

"What was that?"

"Mary Margaret's killer," he replied.

Vicky's patience was wearing thin. "And who was that?"

"Why, old Reverend Lesson. The old fool was in the graveyard carrying a lantern, a rope, and a shovel. Why would he need those items if not to murder poor Mary Margaret?"

Vicky straightened. "Are you certain it was him? Would it not have been to him Lord Gerard was speaking when you heard his voice coming from the neighboring cottage?"

Lord Faegan shook his head. "I have no idea who was in the cottage with Gerard, but I saw the vicar with my own eyes. He was whistling and singing, which he always does when he has been overindulging. I thought little of it at the time; it was nothing more than the foolish ways of an old man. Yet, when I heard about the murder of Mary Margaret, it occurred to me that perhaps he is not as foolish as I once thought him to be. No, Miss Parker, he took Mary Margaret's life if you ask me."

If what this man said was true, Reverend Lesson had lied to her about more than she had first believed. And to whom could the baron have been speaking inside the vicar's cottage if the vicar was not there?

"And you are certain you saw no one else when you left?"

"No one," the earl replied. "The curtains of my carriage were drawn, and I was in deep thought. After all, I had been spurned. I returned here and went straight to bed. The next day, I learned that Mary Margaret had been murdered." He raised his glass as if to toast. "May she be at peace and have forgiven me for the words I spoke to her."

Vicky frowned. "What did you say?"

"Mary Margaret asked me about love," he said in a sad tone. "I told her that love was for poets. Now that she is gone, I wonder if it does truly exist and I missed my only chance to experience it."

Vicky stood. "I thank you for taking the time to speak with me," she said. "Perhaps the murderer will be caught and brought to justice so her soul may rest."

The earl narrowed his eyes for a moment. "I would beware of the type of questions you ask, Miss Parker. I have no issue with them, but there are some out there who will not appreciate your nosing into their business. It is as I said before – some will do anything to learn the location of that treasure. Mary Margaret sadly learned that truth."

"I appreciate the advice and will be careful," she said.

What the earl had told her might have been mostly true, but she was certain there were also a few lies sprinkled in with them. Whether he told them to protect himself or someone else, she was unsure, but she would learn which it was soon enough.

Chapter Nine

"Oh, Vicky," Laura Grant called from the doorway of her millinery shop, which sat next door to the accounting office, "I've the most wonderful news I'd like to share with you. Do you have time for a chat?"

In her mid-thirties and a proud spinster, Laura was Vicky's closest friend, and although she had looked forward to returning home to rest after the day's events, she always made time to have a chat with Laura.

Plus, who knew what James and Percy were up to at that moment? The thought of potatoes with forks protruding from them appeared in her mind and she decided that, indeed, speaking with Laura beforehand was much more appealing.

"Of course," Vicky replied. "I always have time."

"Come inside and I'll put up the closed sign so we needn't worry about anyone listening in."

Vicky followed her friend into the shop and waited for her to lock the door. Laura hurried to the counter that held the many books of plates for clients to peruse, mumbling to herself.

"I haven't made any decision as of yet, but I believe I may go." Laura paused and frowned. "No, I'll think more on it. Yes, that's what I must do, think more on it." She turned to Vicky. "Regardless, this is cause for celebration!"

Vicky scrunched her brow as Laura disappeared behind a curtained doorway. "I am sorry," she called out after her friend, "but where are you going exactly? Have you decided to go away on holiday?"

Laura reappeared with a bottle of wine and two glasses. "Oh, forgive me," she said as she placed the items on the counter and opened the wine bottle. "I've been so excited that I can't seem to keep my thoughts straight. I received word that a well-established and predominant millinery in Folkestone must close their doors. Some sort of family dispute after the proprietor, a Mrs. Jensen, passed away.

"Well, that does not matter. The fact is they have decided to sell the business and I've been given the opportunity to move my shop there!" She poured them each a glass of wine and handed Vicky one, but she did not stop her rush of words. "The question is, do I remain here in London and continue to run only this single shop, or do I use my savings and take over that shop as a second? I've been offered a loan to make up the difference between what I have and what I need – I'll be purchasing everything within the shop, as well. All of the straw, the ribbons, the silk flowers, everything! – but do I wish to go into debt so I may eventually make more money?"

Vicky frowned. Who had offered to loan her money? As a woman, it was unlikely a bank, which meant it was a man. But was he a trustworthy man? It was sad to consider, but most men willing to loan a woman money typically wanted something beyond monetary payment.

Laura did not give her the opportunity to ask. "If I do purchase it, I must decide if I should remain here and employ someone to run that shop. Yet if I decide to go to the Folkestone location, I'll have to take on someone to run this one! Either way, I've been given the chance to expand my business, and I've no idea if I should do it or not! Oh, Vicky, I'm beside myself with excitement, but I must invoke your wisdom. What do I do?"

"How wonderful that you have been given such a wonderful opportunity," Vicky said. "When did you learn of this?" She was genuinely surprised her friend had not mentioned it beforehand. Laura never kept anything from her.

"Just this morning," came Laura's response. "Though I've been in correspondence with Caroline for a number of months now – she is the owner of the Folkestone shop, or rather one of the daughters of the owner.

Anyway, I received a letter by courier this morning, and she and her sister would like to make the first offer to me! Is it not the most amazing thing you've ever heard in your life?" She downed her wine in one gulp. "What should I do?"

Vicky studied her friend. "Would you like me to be honest?"

Laura nodded adamantly. "Yes, of course."

"Then I would like you to remain here. You are my closest friend, and I would miss you terribly if you were to leave. Your shop has grown over the years, and despite the small matter with Miss Brooks...well, perhaps Miss Brooks dying in your shop was not a small matter, but you understand my meaning. Besides that, your business is thriving. Then again, you have spoken time and again about wanting to live near the sea, and this will provide you the perfect opportunity to do just that."

Folkestone was a small seaside village on the southeastern coastline of Kent with a pronounced shipping presence, and with shipping owners came wealthy shipping wives, all of whom would be in need of new hats. It did sound a wonderful opportunity, much to Vicky's chagrin. Yet she truly did want Laura to remain where she was. After all, who would she go to when she needed a ready ear?

Vicky sighed. That was selfish of her. What Laura needed was advice that would be best for her and her business, not what was best for Vicky.

"I assume you have a deadline of some sort to make your decision."

Laura nodded. "Caroline and her family won't officially close for another four months, but she's requested that I give her an answer within a month so she's able to place the business on the market on a more official level if I decline."

As often as this woman had helped her, Vicky hoped she could return the favor. "Here is what I suggest you do. Leave Beatrice in charge here and go to Folkestone for a week. Speak with Caroline, walk along the shops that are in the area, and enjoy the sea. But do not look at your surroundings as a visitor but as a potential resident. Learn if you will be happy living there. By the end of the week, I believe you will have the answer you seek."

"Beatrice is quite capable of being here on her own, and I do trust her." Her mouth twisted in thought. "Yes, I think that's a brilliant idea. I can also see what I think of those who will be my neighbors once I'm there. Now that you've helped me with my problem, what have you been up to these days? I've seen very little of you lately."

"Did I mention that James's Aunt Miriam is in London?"

"You didn't," Laura replied with great interest. "I imagine she's a lovely woman to have had a hand in raising someone like James."

Vicky snorted. "You would think so," she replied. She went on to explain her few, yet significant, interactions with the older woman and then sighed. "Every single word she speaks is in judgment. She even accused me of seducing James!"

Laura gasped. "She didn't!"

"Oh, yes, she very well did. Not only has she determined that she will be in charge of our wedding – which has not even been mentioned in any of our conversations, mind you – but she also suggested that I should no longer be associated with the accounting office once I have taken his name!"

"Why on earth would she do that?" Laura demanded.

"She firmly believes that a married woman should not work. As far as I am concerned, she is no better than our male clients!"

Laura clicked her tongue sympathetically and poured Vicky another glass of wine, this time filling the glass. "And what does James say about this? Surely he doesn't agree, does he?"

"I believe he is torn," Vicky replied. "On one hand, he has come to my defense, albeit rarely. On the other, he also wants to placate his aunt. What he does not understand is that when he does, he only empowers her more. I am at a loss as to what to do. She has scheduled activities for the next two weeks, and I am afraid I will lose my temper with her before the first week is finished!"

"Would that be a bad thing?" Laura asked with a mischievous grin.

"On the surface, no. Yet James thinks a lot of her, so I do not want him to become angry with me, but neither do I want him to feel as if he must choose between us. Argh! That woman is so infuriating!"

"I have an idea," Laura said, a thoughtful expression on her face.

"Bring her here to purchase a hat on one of the days she has scheduled time with you. I'll keep her so distracted with conversation that you'll be able to slip away."

Vicky laughed. "Although the idea is inviting, what will I do on the other days?"

Laura frowned. "I could hire a man to kidnap you," she suggested. "He can take you to a country inn where you can stay until she leaves. Yes, that may just work. When she's gone, you can return. What do you think? Shall I go in search of him today? I can make certain he's handsome if you prefer."

"It is tempting, but that would force me to be away from work and I would not like to cause anyone unnecessary worry, so I must refuse your offer. But I do appreciate your attempts to help."

"You love James, don't you?"

Vicky nodded. "Indeed. Very much so."

"Then I'm afraid you must endure the woman's company until she leaves of her own accord," Laura said with a resigned sigh. "If James thinks so highly of her, it'll do you no good to become argumentative with her. All you'll end up doing is upsetting him and making your time with her all the more unbearable."

"I suppose you are right," Vicky said. "I will do my best to be amicable to her for James's sake." An image of him appeared in her mind, sending a flutter to her heart.

Laura gave her a tiny smile. "Since the two of you professed your love for one another, you smile more often and I've caught you more than once staring at him with a tenderness that wasn't there before."

"I do not stare at him," Vicky insisted. "Well, I suppose I do at times. He is rather handsome, after all. Yet, it is more than that. It is the way he looks when he is deep in thought. Or how his eyes crinkle when he laughs." She frowned. "But his table manners have worsened as of late."

This sent both of them into fits of laughter.

A knock at the door made them turn to find Richard Kent peering through the window, his usual mischievous grin on his face.

"The very gall of that man to bother me again," Vicky said. "I wonder what he wants with me now."

"And what makes you think that you're the only person he calls on?" Laura asked with indignation. "He's here to see me. We've a meeting."

"With you?" Vicky's jaw dropped. Richard was a known thief and a man who was always on the run for one misdeed or another. The idea of that rogue misusing her friend was more than she could bear. "I do not mean to get into your business, Laura, and I would never judge you, but you are not...romantically involved with him, are you? Please, do not fall for his charm. He has used it on too many unsuspecting women to count!"

"Romance with Richard Kent?" Laura asked with a laugh. "I can assure you, I wouldn't even consider such a relationship with that man."

Then Vicky recalled Laura mentioning being offered a loan, and she narrowed her eyes.

Not while I have something to say about it! Vicky thought.

When Laura unlocked the door and Richard entered the shop, Vicky slipped in front of her friend and pushed a finger into Richard's chest.

Richard took a surprised step back, stopping with his back against the door. "What has come over you, woman?" he asked, looking down at her finger as if it were some sort of weapon. "Do not tell me you believe yet another of the silly rumors circulating about me. Have you not learned that you cannot believe everything you hear?"

"Your business is your own," she said with her most menacing snarl, "but Laura is a dear friend of mine."

"Ah! I see!" Richard said with a chuckle. "Your jealousy has finally gotten the best of you, has it? Does Kensington know? If you are willing to forgo the reading of the banns, we can make haste to a vicar I know who will marry us within the week!"

Despite how much this man could frustrate her at times, Vicky could not help but laugh. "The stories you tell yourself are much more entertaining than those written in books."

"That was funny. But you know I only tease. Now, why not explain what has raised your hackles this time?"

"You offering Laura a loan," she snapped. "I trust the terms are reasonable for both of you."

"Of course they are," he replied. "I only seek to—"

Vicky poked him in the chest again. "Do not lie to me, Mr. Kent. Will she come to regret this decision?"

He gave her a wounded look. "You know I would never make an iniquitous offer to someone like Miss Grant. The terms are simple and the interest fair. I am not as unethical as you believe me to be."

Vicky drew in a calming breath. What was it about this man that agitated her so? He had always treated her kindly, after all. Or rather decently in comparison to other men of his ilk. Yet, with his reputation, the idea of Laura being taken in by him was more than she could stand.

She sighed. "I only am concerned for her wellbeing. I meant no offense."

"All is forgotten," Richard said with a wide grin as he stepped past her into the shop. Then he stopped and turned back to her. "Oh, I nearly forgot. Do you remember that baron who was at the home of the Duke of Everton several months ago? Gerard was his name. Lord Gerard. I heard his sister was murdered."

"I heard as much," Vicky replied carefully. "Strangled from my understanding."

Richard frowned. "She was. How did you learn that bit of information?"

"I imagine the same way you did," she replied offhandedly. "Is not everyone talking about it?"

He narrowed his eyes. "Not even the papers have released all the details, including her manner of death. Gerard must be paying them handsomely to keep the particulars about the case quiet."

She shrugged. "Gossip travels faster than most coaches these days."

He glanced from one side to the other and lowered his voice. "There is a rumor that she knew of a hidden treasure buried somewhere in the churchyard where she had been staying when she died."

The last thing she needed was Richard prying into the case when she was attempting to solve it! "I am sure that is pure conjecture," she said. "I would guess that the murderer spread that rumor himself to take any suspicion off of him. Surely you are not falling for it, are you?"

"No, of course not," he said as he opened the door. "I stopped by to say that I must reschedule our meeting, Miss Grant. I have business I must attend to." He lifted his hat and bowed. "Ladies." Then he left the shop.

Vicky looked at Laura, who shrugged.

When she returned to the office, Vicky found James and Percy gone. Good, she would be able to lie down and take a short nap.

As Vicky lay on the bed, her thoughts turned to Laura. The idea of her friend leaving saddened her, but if that was what she wished to do, she would support her. She hoped her suggestion that Laura go to Folkestone for the week would convince her that she preferred London. After all, the seaside would always be there.

She soon drifted off to sleep and dreamed of searching for buried treasure.

Chapter Ten

Vicky spent the following afternoon with Percy, who spent the entire time talking nonstop about a variety of topics. Currently, he was explaining his fascination with spiders, the one creature on this earth that Vicky found the most terrifying. Granted, she did not think much of any bugs, but just the thought of a spider made her insides twist into knots.

"They seem to like me," he was saying as he sat at the kitchen table. "And I like 'em, too. It's why when I get older, I'm goin' to open a museum jus' for them. No need to waste space with all that art and whatnot. Jus' spiders. An' maybe frogs. All sorts of bugs and creatures. An' everyone can come an' learn about 'em. Wouldn't that be wonderful, Miss Vicky?"

Vicky swallowed hard. "Very interesting," she replied, although she spilled her tea, her hand shook so terribly. "But do you not think that they would miss their homes?" The suggestion had worked in the past and she hoped it would now, as well.

"I don' think so," he replied, his nose crinkled in thought. "Not if I bring all their families with 'em."

Thoughts of Percy growing to adulthood brought a twinge of sadness to her heart. And with those thoughts came the reminder of the offer Lord Gerard had given her for finding his father's long-lost treasure. It was about time she presented the idea to Percy.

"You enjoy our lessons, do you not?" she asked.

Percy nodded. "I do like 'em, Miss Vicky. They make me feel clever knowin' I can spell an' read some words. I can't wait to write me own name."

Her heart went out to the boy. "I cannot wait, either," she said, smiling. "Soon, you will be able to read all sorts of books, write letters if you so wish, and work sums. You would like that, would you not?" Again, he nodded, and she considered how to broach the subject of school. Few boys in Percy's situation were given the opportunity to attend any sort of classes, but to be sent away to a boarding school was an entirely different matter. "Did you know that there are schools young boys may attend?"

Percy nodded and leaned back in his chair, sighing dramatically. "They're called boring schools. Rich boys go there to get bored."

Vicky laughed until her sides ached. "They are called boarding schools," she corrected when she could breathe again. "And they are named as such because boys stay there, or are boarded there, during the course of their education. There, they learn all sorts of skills and gather a great deal of knowledge. What do you think of that?"

He pursed his lips and knitted his brows in thought. "What do they do when they've learned everything?"

"Well, they can secure positions doing what very few are able to do. Those boys typically become great businessmen."

Percy's face lit up. "I could learn 'ow to open me museum! I bet they teach that, don' they, Miss Vicky?"

Vicky nodded. "Most certainly."

Then his face fell. "But I'd 'ave to live there?"

"You would, but you are allowed visitors, and the boys return home various times throughout the year."

He slowly rose from his chair, frowning, and placed his hat on his head. "I 'spose I like the idea, but I can't leave ye 'ere alone, now can I? Can I go play?"

"Yes, you may, but be home by five."

"All right, Miss Vicky!" Percy called over his shoulder as he bounded out of the room.

Smiling, Vicky took a sip of her tea. Percy would not be old enough to go away to school for at least another year, so there was no need to press the matter further. She would paint a rosy picture for him, and by the time the day came when he would leave, he would be excited rather than melancholy. Though the idea made her heart hurt.

Her thoughts turned to James and she wondered when he would return from his outing with his aunt. At least the woman had not insisted she go with them.

With a sigh, she closed the book from which she instructed Percy and returned it to the shelf. The boy was making progress, and she was confident that by the end of the year, he would be competent in arithmetic and writing. Reading was still a struggle, but he would come around soon enough.

She went to the front window and peered outside. Then she smiled when she saw James walking up to the front door.

"I have the most wonderful news!" he said as he hung his hat on a peg beside the door. "Aunt Miriam is going to help us."

"Help us?" Vicky asked, her stomach clenching. Now what had that woman suggested? "Help us how?"

"I mentioned that we will be expanding the business," he said, "and she made an excellent point. With the storage room now being used as an office, we will quickly outgrow this place. If we wish to add more employees, we have only the upstairs available, which will then leave us with nowhere to live once we are married. And my flat is just the right size for one man, but an entire family? Not at all."

Vicky sighed. Indeed, his aunt was nosing too far into their business. "James," she said, choosing her words carefully, "you know I love you, but I am not ready to plan a wedding. This inquest into the murder of Mary Margaret Gerard is keeping me quite occupied as it is, besides our usual business. And the idea of a woman I do not know helping—" When James frowned, she realized she had gone too far, so she sighed and said, "Once you and I have come to a decision, I would love to discuss our wedding with her."

A twinge of guilt hit her, for she had no intention of doing such a thing, yet keeping James happy was far more important to her.

"You are right," James said. "We will only discuss the matter when the time is right for you." He took hold of her hands. "Nonetheless, one day this office will become much too crowded and you will need a new home. It is incontrovertible."

The thought of leaving the home in which she had lived all her life did not sit well with Vicky. In fact, it frightened her no end. "A new home?" she asked. "James, here is more than adequate for our needs. We have a perfectly good home, and it is far better than most have. Entire families live in fewer rooms."

He smiled down at her. "Yes, it is adequate for our needs now, but one day, it will become too small. Aunt Miriam has assured me that she will see that we have the necessary funds help us to secure a new house. It is to be her wedding gift to us! Is that not a wonderful gesture?"

The world began to spin, and Vicky pulled away. "I suppose she has chosen the perfect location," she said, doing her best to keep her tone even.

James nodded. "There are houses near Regent Street. Aunt Miriam believes we will be happy there. Can you imagine living in that area of London? We could not be luckier!"

"Do you not like it here?" she asked, hoping she would not hurt his feelings.

"Oh, I do. Your home is lovely, but it lacks sufficient space in which to raise a family. Plus, would it not be better to separate our living space from the business? And Regent Street! Just think, we could build the business to the point that we are able to employ a butler and servants, maybe even a cook!"

Vicky shook her head. Just two weeks ago, James had doled out a large amount to gift her with a lovely meal at the Royal Mayfair, but she did not want to live such an extravagant life. How would they be able to keep up with such expenditures? And servants? She was quite capable of maintaining a house and working at the same time. "James, we have no need for servants, nor a large house."

"Perhaps not now," he replied. "But Aunt Miriam said that husbands should not allow their wives to work; their time would be better spent relaxing and enjoying the luxuries money can buy."

He placed his hands on her shoulders. "Do you not see? I want the best for you. To go shopping whenever you please without concern for what you spend. To be able to see something you would like to purchase and to have the funds to make that purchase. After all you have done, all the work you have put into the accounting firm, the late nights spent with your nose in ledgers, you deserve to have time for yourself."

Although she knew he meant well, Vicky also knew he was not thinking clearly. All she needed in life was for James to continue to love her as he did. The rest was simply excess.

"Will you not at least consider it?" he asked. "Promise me you will."

Vicky gazed up at him. "I will think about it, but I cannot make any promises that I will agree."

"Just you wait and see," he said as he walked to the large desk. "With the business expanding, you will soon be able to afford things you have been deprived of your entire life."

As Vicky returned her gaze out the window, she considered those things of which she had been deprived, and they amounted to nothing. Her father had loved and watched over her with great care, and now James was doing the same. She had a roof over her head and plenty of food to eat, and although her clothes were not fine enough for parties given by the aristocracy, she was clothed. What she feared the most was that Miriam was changing his views of what was important in life, which could never be purchased in a shop.

Chapter Eleven

Vicky shook her head. The way Andrew Thompson's wife clung to him and sobbed into his shoulder Monday morning, one would have believed he was embarking on a journey far from London never to return.

"Now, do not upset them," Jenny Thompson said, sniffling as she pulled away, "and do whatever is asked of you without hesitation. If they require you to leave London for any reason, know that you may, though it would pain me terribly to be away from you for even a single night."

Mr. Thompson was red to his ears. "Jenny, please," he whispered, "you are embarrassing me. And I do not want to be late for my first day!" He turned to Vicky. "I am ready to begin, Miss Parker. Where would you like me to go?"

Vicky had prepared a bit of teasing for him, much like the banter she shared with James, and considered asking him to go to Paris, but after the spectacle she had just witnessed, she thought better of it.

"James has readied a desk for you, so please go inside and he will help you settle in."

With a nod, Mr. Thompson gave his wife one last smile and entered the office.

Vicky turned to the man's wife, who was wiping her nose with a handkerchief. "I imagine you are excited about your husband's new position, but I can see you are also concerned for him.

Is there anything I can do to ease your worries?"

Mrs. Thompson wiped tears from her rosy cheek. "I am worried, Miss Parker. And it is strange; I never had a concern for him before, but his mother," she glanced around them and lowered her voice, "she seems to revel in upsetting me. She recently said things to me that kept me wide awake all last night."

Vicky closed the door behind her and put her arm through that of Mrs. Thompson. "Let us go for a stroll so we may talk. Would you like that?" The younger woman nodded. "Now, tell me what she said that upset you so."

"Last evening, we went to have dinner at Andrew's parents' house. I enjoyed the food, and his father is a pleasant man, but his mother...well, she told me a story about a man who recently lost his position. It caused him undue stress and he turned to alcohol for relief. In no time, he was drinking every night, and it became so bad that eventually all he was doing was nothing more than drinking or sleeping."

"How unfortunate," Vicky said.

Mrs. Thompson nodded. "She then told me that it was my responsibility to see that Andrew stayed on the straight and narrow and encourage him at every turn, for if he were to fail, he would likely become a drunkard and leave me!" She was sobbing again by the time she finished, and Vicky's heart went out to the woman.

"Jenny...may I call you Jenny?"

"Yes, of course," the woman replied.

"I believe your husband is a capable man or I would not have offered him the position. You must trust that he can complete the tasks required of him. It is not your responsibility but rather his. You do trust him, do you not?"

"Yes, of course," Jenny replied. "He is very intelligent, and though he tends to talk too much, he is very kind to everyone he encounters."

"Then there is nothing about which to concern yourself," Vicky said, smiling. "Mothers-in-law have a reputation for being a bit overbearing, but the best way to handle them is to smile, agree with them, and then ignore most of what they say – unless their advice is helpful. You will find doing so will ease the tension between you, which will in turn allow you to sleep peacefully at night."

"You know, you are right," Jenny said firmly. "Thank you, Miss Parker. And I apologize for the spectacle I made outside of your office."

"First of all, you are to call me Vicky. Second, there is no need for apologies. Now, speaking of work, I must return to the office. Unless there is something else you would like to discuss."

"No, but thank you," Jenny replied. "I think I will return home and perhaps enjoy a cup of tea and talk with my neighbor."

Vicky wished the young woman a good day and made her way back the way from where they had come. As she approached, she noticed a carriage parked in front of the office. They were not expecting a client this morning as far as she knew, but that did not mean one did not stop by without warning. In fact, few made appointments ahead of time.

She hung her cloak on its peg and began to untie her bonnet, but a familiar voice made her groan inwardly.

"When a man returns home from work," Miriam was saying, "he should take some time to have a drink at a nearby tavern. A woman should know that her place is at home, so she should not be angry if you return later than your usual time. You must establish these habits and expectations early in your marriage. If you wait too long, you will find her less malleable."

"Habits and expectations?" Mr. Thompson asked. "Such as?"

"Why, any rights a man deserves," Miriam replied. "I already mentioned his right to a drink or two at a tavern, but there are games of chance, hunting expeditions, and archery contests, just to name a few. You must engage in these activities so you are able to learn which you prefer most. You are still young, after all."

"I will not be able to go to the tavern tonight," Mr. Thompson said. "I promised Jenny that we would eat dinner and then take a stroll through the park before dark."

Miriam sniffed. "Nonsense, my boy. Your wife will come to understand that a man needs time to enjoy himself and his activities. I will not lie, I did not like it myself when my husband and I first married, but I soon became accustomed to the rules set before me."

"I am still uncertain…" Andrew mumbled.

Vicky had heard enough. "Mr. Thompson...Oh, hello, Miriam. What a pleasant surprise. I did not expect you until much later this afternoon. I thought you were dropping by closer to closing time."

"That would be my fault," James said, smiling. "Aunt Miriam wanted to surprise you with a trip to the dressmakers so you can have a dress made for the tea with her friends, and she had bound me to secrecy."

Taking a calming breath, Vicky hid her clenched fists in her skirts. "That is a lovely offer, but I am afraid I have much to do today. This is Mr. Thompson's first day, and—"

"Do not be silly," Miriam interrupted. "James can see to Mr. Thompson." She turned to that man. "You are here to work, are you not?"

Mr. Thompson nodded. "I am."

"There, you see," she said, her smile widening. "It is, after all, why you hired him – to give yourself some much-needed freedom. Now, James is quite capable of taking care of the man's training and can be trusted here alone. You do trust him, do you not?"

Please tell me I did not give such a meddlesome appearance when I asked that very question of Jenny! Vicky thought.

She swallowed hard. Should she tell this madwoman that it was none of her business? Yet, she did trust James. By refusing her invitation, would he see it as if she did not trust him?

She stifled a giggle as she considered a bit of playacting. She could begin to sob and confess that she never trusted James; that would send the old woman into a state of shock!

No, Vicky was not a child.

Before she could respond, James said, "Victoria does trust me." How Vicky despised that he called her that! "And a day of leisure is a wonderful idea. It would be entertaining, I am sure. I did not mention it before because it was to be a surprise. I hope you do not mind."

What Vicky wanted to say was that she would rather go to the millinery, take a handful of pins, and poke each of them into her arm than spend the day with his aunt. Yet she could not in good conscious say that to him.

Only two weeks, she reminded herself. *You can do this for two weeks.*

"I could not think of a better way to spend my day," she said, forcing a smile. "Shall we leave now?" The sooner she began this torture, the sooner it would end.

After wishing Mr. Thompson and James a good day, Vicky donned her cloak and bonnet once more and followed Miriam out to the waiting carriage.

"I have a feeling that we will become fast friends, you and I," Miriam said as she stepped into the carriage. "Would you not agree?"

The woman was crafty, Vicky had to admit. Rather than respond with an outright lie, Vicky gave a tiny nod. The carriage pulled away, and Miriam grasped the strap beside her.

"I had great expectations for my James, yet I must admit that his marrying the daughter of an accountant came as a surprise."

"I am sorry I do not meet your stringent criteria in a wife for him," Vicky said, keeping a tight rein on her indignation. "My father was a good man, and I am proud of the firm he built."

Miriam looked at her with surprise. "I did not mean it as an insult toward you or your father, Victoria," she said. "James did say what a wonderful man your father was. My deepest condolences for his death."

Perhaps the woman was not as fiendish as Vicky believed. "Thank you. And he was."

"James told me your father was quite brilliant. I can see now that he passed that gift on to you. And such a rare gift coupled with your beauty..." Miriam sighed. "You are truly a very lucky woman."

Why does she not always speak like this? Vicky wondered. There was kindness in her words, and Vicky considered that, deep down, Miriam was a good person.

"May I ask which dressmaker we will be visiting today?" Vicky asked.

"Regent Street," Miriam replied. "Madam Beauchêne is the finest dressmaker in all of London. Now, it is not easy to make an appointment with her, but I have my connections. After all, you will need something appropriate to wear when we meet with my friends for tea. We certainly cannot have you go in what you are currently wearing, now, can we?"

Vicky sat stunned as Miriam took her by the hand. "Victoria, please indulge an old woman an afternoon of shopping. At the very worst, you order a new dress. At the best, we find a common bond that will bring us closer together. What do you say?"

"Yes, of course, that would be nice," Vicky replied. Inside she was not as sure.

A bond? she thought. *Oh, yes, I am sure that will happen.* The words dripped with sarcasm, but she could not seem to think them any other way.

Miriam patted her hand. "Good."

What the woman said was true; at least Vicky would receive a new dress, and that could never be a bad thing. Could it?

Chapter Twelve

Madame Beauchêne's was located between a tailor and a haberdasher on Regent Street. The shop was much larger and more extravagant than Mrs. Cutler's shop on Wellington, and a good thing, too. At least two dozen women flipped through the various books of plates or fingered the fabric swatches fastened to boards that hung from the walls. Three women in matching aprons and simple white mob caps rushed from one area to the next, likely clerks, and when one of them went through a curtained door at the back of the shop, Vicky caught a glimpse of several women sitting hunched over piles of fabric, needles and thread in hand.

One woman in particular caught Vicky's attention. A tall, formidable woman in her late fifties, Madame Beauchêne had dark hair that was pulled back and fastened with a comb. Even with the number of women in the shop, Madame Beauchêne's French accent could be heard above them all.

"Ah, yes, *Madame*," the woman was saying to a stout lady with a hat with so many feathers, Vicky suspected that eggs lay beneath them, "I will see that your gown is ready by then." She paused and tapped her lips. "No, before then. I will put my best seamstresses on it immediately!"

The stout woman left wearing a pleased smile.

"Madame Beauchêne truly does make the finest dresses in all of London," Miriam whispered. "They may cost a fortune, but you will see they are well worth the price paid."

"It is kind of you to bring me here," Vicky said, "but I am sure the cost is well above my budget. And I cannot accept such an expensive gift from you. Plus, where would I wear something so extravagant?"

Miriam's click of her tongue came as no surprise. "I spoke to James yesterday, and I informed him that a husband's duty is to be his family's provider. Once he understood that he would be responsible for purchasing everything a lady needs, he insisted on giving me money to pay for today's purchases." She leaned in closer and lowered her voice. "There is no need to worry about the cost. James has agreed that he will be responsible for seeing you have all you need to take your place in society once you are married."

Vicky sighed. Society indeed! If she and James were to marry, they would still be accountants. And accountants did not wear fancy clothes or receive invitations to parties given by the *ton*! The next two weeks were going to be unbearable, she was sure of it.

"When I lived in London in my younger years, I often shopped here." Miriam's voice had a dreaminess to it. "Then Stephen passed on..."

"I am sorry for your loss," Vicky said sincerely. "James has spoken highly of his uncle."

"He was a good man," Miriam said. "Granted, he was quite busy with work and other matters a majority of the time, but he did all he could to assure that I received everything I wanted. I found solitude in coming here and spending his money." She winked, and Vicky could not help but give a small laugh. "Now that he is gone, I have plenty of money, and I wish to share it with others." She heaved a heavy sigh. "Perhaps I am wanting nothing more than to find that happiness here again – an old woman's attempt at sentimentality. I should not expect you to suffer through it with me. Come, we may leave if you wish."

A terrible sense of guilt washed over Vicky and she could not stop blurting, "No, we may remain. It will be a nice diversion from the typical. Furthermore, a simple dress will please both me and James." She stressed the word "simple". If she was not careful, Miriam would have her fitted for a ball gown worthy of a court appearance!

"Wonderful!" Miriam said.

"Ah, *madame* Kensington, it is so good to see you again!" Madame Beauchêne said in her French accent as she kissed Miriam on each cheek. "It has been much too long since you visited us." She gave Miriam a frown. "I do not recognize this dress. Tell me you have not found a new dressmaker!"

"I was in need of something in a hurry," Miriam replied. "But rest assured that it was a one-time purchase."

Madame Beauchêne turned to Vicky. "Did you find a new lady's maid?" she asked. "Did your lovely Silvia get married after all?"

Vicky's cheeks burned as she glanced down at her dress. Lady's maid? Surely she did not wear something that one would mistake for a uniform!

Miriam laughed. "No, this is my soon-to-be niece-in-law, Miss Victoria Parker. As you can see, she tends more toward a simpler and plain look. We will need your help to see that she is dressed in the latest fashion. But can you have at least one of the dresses completed by next Monday? I realize it is very short notice, but—"

Madame Beauchêne raised a hand. "Say no more, *Madame*. I can see myself there is need for *urgence*. I assume you are willing to cover the extra cost of paying my girls for remaining later than usual?"

"Of course," Miriam replied as if this were expected.

"Excellent! I will leave you to look through the plates. When you are ready to order…Ah, but you know exactly what to do, *Madame*!" she added a laugh to the last.

"I do," Miriam replied. "I will signal when we have made our choices."

"*Très bien, Madame*," Madame Beauchêne replied before leaving them alone.

Miriam was already flipping through one of the nearby books, and she stopped at one in particular. "This will look lovely on you," she said.

Vicky looked where the woman pointed. "Indeed, it is a beautiful dress, but is it not a bit…impractical?" She pointed to another plate in a book beside the one before them. "Would this not be more sensible?"

Miriam clicked her tongue. "I have seen maids wear finer dresses. It is no wonder you are mistaken for a lady's maid when you choose clothing so simple. No, I think this one would be much better suited to the woman marrying my James."

"Perhaps," Vicky said, choosing her words carefully, "but do you not believe it is not too...revealing?" She eyed the low neckline. How could she wear a dress like this in an office where men were the primary clients?

"Not at all," Miriam replied. "The latest fashions do show a bit more décolletage than the former, but all the ladies are wearing them these days, are they not, Madame Beauchêne?"

"*Oui, Madame,*" Madame Beauchêne replied. "That is true."

Of course she would agree! She was making a fortune off this purchase alone!

"Be that as it may," Vicky said firmly, "I believe we should look at some other plates. I simply would not feel comfortable donning something like this one."

"Of course, my dear," Miriam said with a smile. "After all, you will be the one wearing it. I was merely voicing my opinion."

Vicky was momentarily stunned. She had expected the woman to argue further; it was a pleasant relief that she had respected Vicky's wishes. Perhaps Miriam had been right in her prediction for the day – they would have a pleasant time together. In fact, the woman was becoming more tolerable as the day wore on.

After carefully selecting two more dresses – Miriam had insisted Vicky purchase three to save her from needing to return anytime soon – they eyed the various fabric choices. She chose a cream muslin for the simpler of the dresses, a woven light-blue cotton fabric with tiny pink and yellow printed flowers and lace on the neckline and sleeves for the second, and a white cotton with roller-printed red flowered fabric for the bottom hemline on the final dress.

Once the decisions were made, Madame Beauchêne said, "Please follow me, Miss Parker. I will have Bette measure you. She comes from Paris, from the very area where I was born! You will find she is quick and efficient; just what one needs when taking measurements, no?"

Bette was a pleasant girl of perhaps eighteen with rosy cheeks and dark eyes, and as promised, she worked quickly.

"Do not be nervous, *mademoiselle*," the girl said as she took up a measuring tape from a table. "This will not take long."

Bette mumbled as she worked rather than making conversation, making notations on a tiny pad until she took the last measurement. It suited Vicky just fine.

"There we are. You see? Not long at all."

"Thank you," Vicky said, her cheeks hot as she donned her dress once more. She was not accustomed to standing in nothing more than her shift. It was bad enough whenever she saw Mrs. Cutler, and she had been going there for her dresses for years.

When Vicky returned to the main section of the shop, Miriam was speaking with Madame Beauchêne, her voice filled with sadness. "When Stephen died, I thought my life no longer had meaning," she was saying. "Yes, I had James to watch over and instruct, and that did bring me peace, but when I left London, he decided to remain."

She smiled as Vicky walked up to them. "Then I met Victoria, and I again have someone I may guide. Now, do not misunderstand me, Victoria is a capable woman, but she lacks understanding as to what a marriage should truly entail. After all, she lost her mother at a very young age. What does a man know of what is required of a woman? But she has no need for concern, for I will always be here to do my part, even in the years to come."

Madame Beauchêne nodded her approval. "You cannot have a more fitting *pédagogue, Mademoiselle. Madame* Kensington will make you a better woman, I am sure of it."

Alarm bells rang in Vicky's mind. "But I am content with who I am," she said. "I do not need to change."

Miriam laughed. "Ah, the stubbornness of youth," she said, shaking her head. "Well, Madame Beauchêne, we must be on our way. I will be sure to stop by again before I leave."

"See that you do," Madame Beauchêne said, kissing Miriam's cheeks again before doing the same to Vicky. "And I do hope you will become a regular client, *mademoiselle*."

Vicky made a noncommittal mumbling Madame Beauchêne seemed to accept as affirmation and followed Miriam outside.

"I do not know about you," Miriam said, "but I am famished. Oh, and I scheduled an appointment with a woman who will be able to give you instruction in poise and posture. If she has time, I would also like her to teach you how to do embroidery. I imagine you never had the opportunity to learn how to use a needle seeing as how you had no mother to guide you. After all, you must have a lady-like activity to fill your days once you and James are married. Needlework is a must-know for any lady."

Vicky came to a stop. "Miriam, I am thankful for our outing today. It has been a truly wonderful experience."

"But of course," Miriam said, gushing. "We will soon be family. I never had a daughter, but I will now have the benefit of having you."

Despite the woman's kind words, Vicky knew she had to put a stop to this before it got too far, and she had always felt that being direct was the best way to handle most uncomfortable situations. "I appreciate you wishing to work with me, but I must politely decline your offer of assistance. My name and character are virtually unblemished, and I have no need for instruction on how to walk and stand – I do both quite competently. As for marriage, James and I have yet to discuss the prospect. Even so, I would like us to control what he and I do once we are wed."

Miriam brought a hand to her breast. "I have never been so insulted in my life," she gasped. "Why do you hate me so?"

"I do not hate you," Vicky said, doing her best to keep her tone pleasant despite her annoyance. "But my life, and that of James, is ours, not yours. I had hoped our time together today would not come to this, but I thought it best to be honest with you. I do hope you understand."

Miriam raised her head and frowned as she glared down her nose at Vicky. "Very well. I see you for who you truly are. Here I am bearing gifts, and you throw them back in my face. If you prefer not to appreciate that I took the time to schedule training that few women of your station have the opportunity to attend, then so be it."

Vicky stifled a sigh. Perhaps complete honesty had not been the best path in this situation. "I do appreciate your gifts, and one day I hope to be like you – a woman with carefree days and without responsibility. Unfortunately, today is not that day. You see, I have a meeting scheduled soon, one I cannot avoid. May we reschedule the sessions for another day? Remember, this outing was not on the schedule you gave me, so I was unaware we would be away from the office when I planned my day." She offered a warm smile in hopes that her words would pacify the woman.

"Well, yes, of course," Miriam replied. Vicky sighed with relief. Another disaster diverted. "I believe I will remain on Regent Street; it has been far too long since I have been able to visit the shops here. Will you need transportation to where it is you need to go?"

"No, thank you," Vicky replied. "It is close by." She embraced Miriam, which seemed to surprise her. "Thank you for a wonderful day. I regret that we are unable to spend the rest of it together, but I am certain we will have more opportunities to do so before you leave."

Vicky's father had once told her that only fools were quick to display their anger, and she had certainly made a fool of herself.

"One must show kindness in every situation," he had told her. "For by doing so, not only do you avoid arguments, but you also are more likely to get what you want."

Seeing Miriam's pleased expression, Vicky realized how right her father had been.

Chapter Thirteen

Vicky had not lied, not outright, about needing to speak to someone. Granted, it was not a scheduled meeting, but it was a meeting, nonetheless. Of the list of names Lord Gerard had given her, one man could be found at a tavern located two streets from where the dressmaker was located. Whether or not The Forgotten Knight was owned by Mr. Donald Galpin or if he was merely an employee of the tavern remained to be seen.

The facade of the building that housed the tavern was clean and well-kept. The windows sparkled and the paint was fresh. Those who walked past the establishment wore fine clothing. Vicky opened the deep-green door and walked into a space that was far different from the deceptive outside.

At the end of the long bar stood a man in his later twenties with bright unruly red hair, a stained coat, and patched trousers. Despite his disheveled appearance, his voice was mesmerizing. His words, however, were not.

'Twas upon that very night me love died,
And for three days I could do not but cry.
Then I met her cousin Dinah…

He paused for two breaths.

And I thought, 'Sure, I'll give her a try!'

The patrons erupted in laughter and banged their hands on the tables or the bar as the red-haired man gave a deep bow. He took his cap and walked around, collecting coins from the audience, who were more than happy to throw in a copper or two.

"Can I 'elp ye, miss?"

Vicky turned to the barman. "Please. I am looking for Mr. Donald Galpin. That would not be you by chance, would it?"

The man laughed and tugged on the end of one of his long mustaches. "Thank the All Mighty I'm not," he replied. "That's 'im over there." He pointed to the singer, who had taken a seat at a corner table, a mug in front of him. "Yer not 'ere to ask 'im to sing at yer weddin' are ye?"

Vicky laughed. "No. I am here for another matter."

"Good," the barman said as he wiped an empty mug with a rag. "Donald there, 'e's a tendency to like 'is drink too much. Started a fight two months ago when 'e'd been asked to sing at a weddin'. Le's jus' say it didn't go well. 'Tis why I asked."

Vicky thanked the man and walked over to the table where Mr. Galpin sat. "Excuse me, Mr. Galpin. My name is Victoria Parker. May I speak with you?"

He grinned up at her. "Only if you call me Donald. Please, sit. My apologies for my behavior at the wedding if that's why you're here. I tend to drink more than I can handle. Especially when they give it to me free of charge!"

"Donald—"

He raised a hand to forestall her. "When I drink too much, I get angry, and after that foolish butler lied to me, I couldn't stop myself from returning to say a few choice words to him. But don't worry, I won't repeat them in front of a lady." His grin said he likely would if she gave him permission to do so.

"I have no idea about any wedding," Vicky said before he could continue. "I am here to speak to you about Mary Margaret Gerard. I was told you were...an acquaintance of hers?"

Donald leaned back in his chair and closed his eyes. "Ah, Mary Margaret. Yes, such a lovely woman. I still can't believe I was tasked with wooing her. Me, Donald Galpin."

He opened his eyes and laughed before signaling to the barkeep. "Another one, Collins!" He looked at Vicky. "Would you like something?"

"No, thank you."

He shrugged. "Suit yourself. No one believed me when I told them, you know, that the baron offered me money to play the suitor."

"So it is true that her brother hired you for this task?" Vicky asked.

"Oh, it's true," he replied. "He said I was to get her to reveal the location of some treasure, but he didn't seem confident I'd be able to pull it off. I think that's why he hired the lot of us – to give her a bit of variety."

Vicky frowned. "I am afraid I do not understand."

The barkeep walked over and placed a second mug of ale on the table. "Anythin' fer ye, miss?"

She considered responding the same as she had previously but then changed her mind. "Wine please, and another for him, as well. On me." Anything to get the man to tell her everything he knew.

Donald grinned at her. "Well, that's very kind of you, miss."

"My pleasure. Now, you were saying something about Lord Gerard's motives for hiring men to play suitors to his sister?"

"That's simple," Donald replied. "He's been after Mary Margaret to tell him the location of their father's treasure for years. He'd buy her all sorts of gifts – fancy dresses, hats, all those things women like. And then she goes and becomes a spinster!" He barked a laugh and shook his head. "Now, that sure made him angry."

"Why? Because it made him look bad?"

He snorted. "No. It's 'cause she swore to reveal it to the man she loved, or so I gathered from Gerard. You see, he and his sister apparently never got on well. I think Gerard hoped to supply the man she fell in love with so he'd have a direct connection to the man who'd learn where the treasure was. But he didn't hire just any men, he hired the lot of us."

Vicky despised speaking to men who had consumed too much alcohol; they never spoke clearly. "What sort of 'lot' do you mean?"

He laughed again. "A vicar, for one. And me? I make my money singing in taverns! What'll someone like her want with the likes of me? And that Earl, Faegan? He's had more affairs than I've had mugs of ale in my lifetime. Then there's the likes of Haring," he leaned forward and lowered his voice, "a murderer."

Vicky frowned, remembering the names on the list Lord Gerard had given her. "My apologies but Mr. Haring is a murderer?" This would have been important information the baron could have provided at the onset of the inquest! "If that is true, why is he still living? Few murderers sidestep the gallows."

Donald chuckled. "Oh, he hasn't been tried, but rumor has it that he strangled his brother when they were young. He wasn't any more than fifteen at the time. He strangled him with a rope, just like Mary Margaret."

"I see," Vicky said, making a mental note and storing it away. "That is quite helpful. Now, may I ask what happened the night of Miss Gerard's death?"

"Well, she sent word that I was to meet her at ten at night. I was singing here until nine – I made plenty that night so I was able to have a few drinks before I left. When I got to the church in Edgeware, I could hear that old vicar crying like a babe."

"And where was he at this time?" Vicky asked.

"Inside his cottage, the one next to Mary Margaret's," Donald replied. "I could hear another man berating him."

"Could you hear what was being said?" Vicky asked.

"Nah, couldn't make out anything, not with the vicar wailing like he was." He barked a laugh. "How that old man could believe he'd be able to woo someone like Mary Margaret's beyond me. Ah, well, it doesn't matter, really, but I find it humorous all the same. There's not much more to say than that, really. Mary Margaret invited me inside, I had a glass of wine – I can't abide the stuff but she liked it so I drank it anyway. Give me a mug of ale over wine anytime. Then she told me I wasn't the one she'd tell her secret to, so I left."

"I imagine that upset you," Vicky said. "After all, you put in a great deal of hard work trying to win her over, yet there you were, forced to leave without the information you so hoped to gain."

He shrugged. "Not at all. I couldn't have cared less, to be honest. I make plenty of coin here, and it's a much more entertaining way of making money. I knew Mary Margaret could never care for a man like me. I've no wealth or any other means to take care of her. We did get to be close, though. So close, in fact, that I spent a few nights there – me sleeping on her sofa, mind you – 'til that nosy old vicar came poking his nose around, knocking at the door and making excuses to see what we were up to."

"Why bother to make the attempt if you knew she would not choose you?" Vicky asked.

"Mary Margaret liked to listen to my songs," he said with a wide grin. "She'd laugh when I sang them to her." He sighed. "We'd sit for hours just talking, but she'd never spoken about her parents – they're both dead, you know – but that night, she talked about them for the first time."

Surprised, Vicky asked, "Were they fond memories that she shared?"

"Most of it was about her mother," he said. Then he glanced around and lowered his voice. "Apparently, the woman had numerous affairs, and it didn't matter if they were titled men or servants! Mary Margaret said she caught her mother once, and when she told her brother, he berated her for it – his sister, not his mother. But the father wasn't any different. When I worked at the market years ago, he'd stop by and buy flowers from a woman there before leaving town."

The conversation was moving further away from the murder than Vicky liked. She needed to steer it back to the topic at hand. "That is very interesting," she said. "And during your time there with Miss Gerard that night, did you see or hear anything unusual? Besides the vicar sobbing upon your arrival, of course."

The barkeep placed a new mug in front of Donald and scowled. "Ye'd best get to singin' soon. I'm not lettin' ye have any more credit. Ye already owe me over a pound as it is!"

Donald waved the man away. "I'm nearly done here," he growled. The barkeep walked away and Donald shook his head. "Ungrateful lout. I bring a bit of culture into his establishment, and that's how he treats me?"

"As you were saying?" Vicky prodded.

"Oh, yeah, well, when I left, I saw Gerard, that snake of a baron, pacing outside the vicar's cottage. But when I went to collect my horse, I saw something that I didn't even wonder about until I'd ridden several miles and my head had cleared."

"And what was that?"

"Haring and the vicar standing at the gate that leads to the graveyard. There was the old vicar sobbing and singing a tune, a shovel and lantern in his hand, while Haring was shouting at him! The next thing I knew, Haring called him a fool, slapped him across the face, and took the shovel and lantern from him. Old Reverend Lesson ran back to his cottage, still sobbing." He pointed a finger at Vicky and narrowed his eyes. "I tell you, Haring was supposed to be the last one of us to see Mary Margaret, so I bet he's the one who murdered her."

Vicky had much to consider after this meeting, that was certain! She had so many unanswered questions left, but this man would likely not be the one to answer them.

"Did you love her?"

It was quiet for a moment and then Donald stood. "I suppose a man can't help but love Mary Margaret. I'd better get at it before I'm thrown out. Good day to you, Miss Parker."

Vicky nodded and left just as Donald began his next song. She was drawing closer to learning the truth and was more confident she knew the location of the treasure. What bothered her, however, was that she still was unsure who murdered Mary Margaret Gerard, and to her, that was far more important than finding a buried treasure despite what the woman's brother thought.

For now, she had to return home and speak to James about her day with his aunt – a task to which she was not looking forward.

Chapter Fourteen

As soon as Vicky entered the small kitchen at the back of the office, she knew there was going to be trouble. Miriam sat at the table beside James, who was holding her hand.

"Oh, my!" Miriam said with exaggerated surprise. "Victoria is here. I should leave before she becomes angry with me again." She staggered as she tried to stand.

"You do not need to go," James said. "I am certain Victoria would not mind if you stayed."

His calling her Victoria still rankled her, but his aunt's behavior annoyed her far more.

"No," Miriam said. "It was I who was overbearing today. I was trying to make up for lost time, I am afraid. Victoria has every right to send me away. I suppose I deserve to be ostracized. I am always nosing into other people's business, even if it is only to help." Vicky did not miss the sly smile that appeared on the woman's face when James glanced away.

Vicky recalled her father's words once again. "As I said earlier," she said, stifling a sigh, "I enjoyed our outing together, and I look forward to the next outing. James, you should have seen how much Madame Beauchêne respects your aunt. It is clear that her goodwill and kind manners have made her a prominent woman." It was Vicky's turn to give a sly smile. Oh, but how she hated these games!

James smiled. "Aunt Miriam has always done her best to please everyone around her. You see, Aunt Miriam? I told you Victoria likes you. You have been worried for no reason."

Miriam sighed dramatically. "I suppose you are right. Now that I know that I am not intruding, would it be possible to get a cup of tea?"

"Allow me," James said but then stopped when his aunt clicked her tongue. "Or rather, would you make us a pot of tea, Victoria?"

Vicky forced a smile. "I would love to," she replied. Images of tripping and pouring hot water into Miriam's lap crossed her mind.

She shook her head. When had she become such a terrible person? Granted, her temper could rise at times, but the idea of hurting someone was going too far!

This will all soon be over, she reminded herself. *Then life will be back to normal.*

Once the tea was ready, Vicky poured. Then a familiar voice came to her ear.

"Miss Vicky?" Percy called from the vestibule. He marched into the kitchen, his cheeks covered in dust and grime. "Oh, 'ello. Ye must be Auntie Miriam." The boy had been fortunate enough to have yet to deal with the woman.

Do stop that! Vicky said, silently chastising herself. *It is only a fortnight!* That was becoming a mantra.

"Have you been playing in the mud?" Miriam asked.

Percy nodded, his eyes bright. "I 'ave."

Vicky braced herself for the tongue lashing that was sure to come.

"That is simply wonderful!" Miriam said. She stood and pulled Percy into a tight embrace. "Young boys should play all day. I also heard you like frogs, is that true?"

"Oh, yes, missus," Percy replied. "I do like 'em. I wanna open a museum for 'em when I'm bigger."

"And so you should, Percy," Miriam replied as she ruffled his hair. She bent over so she was closer to him. "You know, you can do whatever you wish in life. Do not allow anyone to tell you otherwise. Now, since I will soon be your auntie, how about I take you to get you a few sweets and perhaps a wooden toy. Would you like that?"

Percy gave a vigorous nod to his head. "Oh, yes, I'd like that a lot, missus. Could we go now?"

"Maybe in a while," Miriam replied.

Vicky gave a small laugh. "Yes, in a while, Percy. Aunt Miriam must drink her tea, and you need to go clean up for supper."

"All right," Percy replied. "Nice meetin' ye, missus."

"Is he not absolutely wonderful?" James asked. "Is he not everything I told you and more?"

Miriam returned to her seat. "He is darling," she replied. "But he must be educated. And why do you allow him to spend all day outside playing?"

James shrugged. "It is how he lived his life before we began caring for him. Victoria was reluctant at first, but we discussed it and decided to allow him to continue with what he is accustomed to, within reason."

"Then you have made a poor decision, James," Miriam said with a sniff. "Once a week and no more. Young boys are prone to mischief and you should not encourage it."

"You are wise, Aunt Miriam," James mumbled. "I will surely consider it."

"See that you do. When you do finally decide to marry, he will be your son. The Kensington name cannot be marred by bad behavior. I am trusting you in this matter, James. Do not disappoint me."

James's shoulders slumped. "Yes, Aunt Miriam."

Miriam seemed to ignore him. "You should have seen James in school. He was fond of spending his days with his head in the clouds. You have no idea how many letters I received from the headmaster concerning this problem when he first came to stay with me. With his malady being a burden, he should have been working extra hard to get to where he needed to be."

For the first time since knowing James, Vicky finally understood why he was always so reserved. Miriam was an overbearing, cruel woman who spent entirely too much time chastising him while at the same time acting as if she had his best interests at heart. Well, Vicky was not about to allow it to continue!

Before she could say anything, however, Miriam said, "I do not wish to go, but I imagine Victoria must begin preparations for dinner." She stood and turned to James.

"You should go and enjoy a mug of ale at one of the nearby taverns. I am sure you will have plenty of time before the food is ready."

"Thank you, Aunt Miriam," James said. "I will consider it."

As James walked Miriam to the door, Vicky lowered herself into a chair and dropped her head into her hands. Try as she might, she could not abide that woman! Worse still, Miriam's old influences over James seemed to be returning.

She heard Percy's voice from upstairs and smiled. The boy was likely playing with a handful of rocks he called his "pets". Two nights earlier, he had told Vicky that the rocks were scouring London at night looking for missing treasure.

When James returned, she sat up straighter. "We need to speak."

"We do." He placed a hand on the back of a chair but did not sit. "You heard Aunt Miriam admitting that she was overbearing today. Victoria, you should have seen her when she returned this afternoon! I thought she would burst into tears! But I told her you are a forgiving person and that she had nothing over which to worry."

"But, James, she *is* overbearing! I fear she is trying to influence you in ways that are not for good intentions."

James frowned. "Influence me? What do you mean?"

"I do not appreciate the way she speaks to you, criticizing your every move. She dredges up mistakes you made as a child to shame you. Yet it is more than that. Today, she insisted I purchase not one but *three* new dresses. James, I do not even need one new dress!"

The flicker of sadness that crossed his eyes was like a knife twisting in her heart. "I want you to have nice things," he said. "If there is anyone in this world who deserves them, it is you."

"You have a good heart," she said, smiling, "and the words you speak do more for me than you can ever imagine. As much as I appreciate the gesture, you do not have to buy me things to prove you care for me."

To her shock, he pursed his lips and his jaw tightened. "What you mean to say is that you do not wish me to do anything for you. Very well, I will remain your assistant – in romance as well as in work."

"I did not mean—"

He ignored her attempt to explain. "Any time I mention a future where we have a fine home and you have new dresses or anything else I would like to provide for you, you dismiss me as if I were some sort of fool. That is well enough. We can forever remain here if that is what you would like. Wear the same dresses until they are threadbare. It makes little difference to me. I will no longer argue with you about any of it."

Tears stung Vicky's eyes as she reached out to place a hand on his arm. "I am sorry if I sound ungrateful. I simply do not want you to put an undue burden on yourself by giving me gifts I do not need. If you wish to buy me things, do so. Just promise me that you will not lose sight of what we share. That is what is most important, not the things we have."

James looked down at her, a sad smile on his lips. "What we have is wonderful," he replied. "How could I ever lose sight of you? But as we come closer to marrying, you must understand that things will change. With my aunt's help, we will have a wonderful home, fashionable clothes, all the finest things we desire. That is what I want – to give you all the best life has to offer."

Vicky nodded, although inside she was torn between allowing James to make unnecessary purchases and making certain those purchases did not harm what they shared together. Had they not seen what overspending could do to the accounts of the clients who paid it no mind? How many estates went into ruin because their owners chased after things they did not need?

Yet, as he wrapped his arms around her, she knew they would be all right in the end. Miriam certainly could not ruin what they had in a mere two weeks, could she?

Chapter Fifteen

Vicky had a lovely two-day reprieve from James's aunt Miriam, but the woman returned to spend an additional two hours going once again from shop to shop along Wellington Street. Unfortunately, or perhaps fortunately, Miriam felt the quality of the items in that area were not to her liking and therefore made very few purchases. Percy had joined them, and although she paid little attention to him, Miriam did purchase him a new toy, a wooden spinning top.

They had returned to the office in the early afternoon and Miriam left for her hotel just before the rain began to fall. Now, James sat at the large desk with a client, Mr. Nicholas Dunne, across from him. Vicky sent Percy upstairs to play with his new toy before preparing a pot of tea.

"It is not just matters of business," Mr. Dunne was saying when Vicky returned. "Corruption has crept into every facet of life in London. No, in England! I long for the days when I was a boy, when it was safe and servants could be trusted, as were your own kin." He heaved a heavy sigh. "Those days are regretfully long past."

Seeing a pause in their conversation, Vicky set the tray on the desk.

Mr. Dunne looked up at her and smiled. "Well, Miss Parker, it is so wonderful to see you again."

"Thank you, Mr. Dunne," she replied, pouring a cup of tea and placing it on the desk in front of him. "There we are."

He brought the teacup to his lips and sipped. "Perfect," he said with a smile before it dropped and the frown he had been wearing returned. "Now, where was I? Oh, yes, the travesty of the decline of the nation will be noted in the annals of history, mark my words. In fact, I hope to be mentioned as a champion for saner times."

The man had been a client of Parker Accounting for several years, having trusted his accounts to her father after one meeting. Even then, he spent a majority of his time lamenting the destruction of society as a whole, but more so of London. At times he blamed men, at others, women. If Vicky considered it fully, he blamed nearly every person except himself.

"Speaking of travesty," Mr. Dunne continued, "did you hear about the murder of Mary Margaret Gerard? Apparently, she was killed after enticing a number of men."

Vicky paused. What did this man know about the murder?

"I did," James replied. "But no more than the fact that she had been murdered. Have you heard any significant details about it? They are being rather hush-hush about the whole thing."

Good old James, Vicky thought and she mouthed a silent "Thank you!" at him. She did not miss the tiny upcurve of the corner of his lips.

Mr. Dunne snorted. "Of course I have, Kensington. I know everything that happens in London and the surrounding areas."

Vicky nodded. The man could put the gossip columns to shame!

"It can be difficult to sift through what is truth and what is rumor, of course, but it appears she had at least two suitors who called on her regularly. Even at night and without benefit of a chaperon! She may have been a spinster, but she was unmarried and should not have been entertaining men alone. Even spinsters should be conscientious of convention."

Vicky gave an appropriate gasp and said in her most demure voice, "Mr. Dunne, you are such an intelligent man. Surely you have some idea of who did this terrible deed."

Mr. Dunne sighed dramatically and set his teacup in its saucer. "I must apologize beforehand for what I am about to say, Miss Parker, for a subject so heinous should never be discussed in the company of those of delicate sensibilities.

However, I do know that you were present at many of your father's meetings and therefore can assume that many of those men likely spoke more candidly than they should have."

"Oh, yes," Vicky replied. "I have heard more than any one woman should hear. But I know you speak only what is true, so I am sure I can stomach anything you have to say. After all, if it is the truth, how can I not hear it regardless of its contents?"

"You are so right," Mr. Dunne replied. He leaned forward, and Vicky was reminded of an older woman in a gossip circle. "I heard that the same day poor Miss Gerard was found, a Mr. Christopher Haring left London in quite a hurry. That is highly suspicious if you ask me."

"Are you sure he did not have business to conduct elsewhere?" Vicky asked.

"Ha! Business?" He snorted. "I doubt that. No, I believe he was overcome with guilt for what he did, which was murdering that poor woman."

"But why would he?" Vicky asked with all appearance of innocence.

Mr. Dunne laughed. "Because he was one of the two men who was calling on Miss Gerard!"

Vicky covered her mouth in mock surprise. "No! I hope you do not mind my asking, but how did you learn of this?"

"Why, from the baron himself. He said he went to speak to Haring early that morning before sunrise, they argued, and then Haring left London. Seems as clear as day to me."

"Do you know what they argued about?"

"He did not say and I did not ask. His sister had been murdered, so I did not feel right in asking more than was necessary."

Vicky nodded sympathetically. "Well, I do hope they find the poor woman's killer," she said, collecting the empty teacups and pot. "We certainly do not need a murderer running around London!"

Vicky left the men to their discussion, which had turned into the more famous murders in the country. She had already had her fill of murders with those that she investigated; discussing any that had taken place in the past held no interest to her.

What she had learned from Mr. Dunne, however, did interest her. If it were true that Lord Gerard spoke to Mr. Haring, why had he not mentioned it when enlisting her aid? What had they discussed? And why did Mr. Haring leave London so soon after that encounter?

When she returned to the office, the men were discussing hunting. That was worse than infamous murders! As it was raining, Percy would remain upstairs, playing with his new toy for some time, so she was free to go next door and speak to Laura. She threw a cloak over her shoulders and pulled up the hood before stepping out into the downpour.

The tiny bell above the door to the millinery tinkled as she entered the shop. An older woman in a gray dress and green cloak was finalizing her order with Laura.

"Now, I do trust my hat will be decent," the lady was saying. "I am far too old to be attracting young men, so I do hope my hat is tasteful."

"I can assure you, Mrs. Calens, it will be refined and elegant," Laura replied, the corners of her mouth turning so slightly it was difficult to see if one did not know her well. "I'll see that it's delivered to your home the moment it is ready."

The old woman muttered something unintelligible and then scuttled out of the shop.

"Provocative hats?" Vicky asked as she hung her dripping coat from a peg on the wall beside the door. "I had no idea hats could incite lust. Where do I get mine?"

Laura laughed. "Bless her," she said with a sigh as she leaned both elbows on the counter and dropped her chin into her hands. "Believe it or not, it'll be people like her that will make me miss London. If I leave, that is."

"Have you made a decision?" Vicky asked.

"Not yet," Laura replied, standing once more and organizing the forms that lay before her. "I leave tomorrow for Folkestone as you suggested. By the time I return, I'm likely to have my answer. It really was a brilliant idea, my going there to experience the place." She tilted her head and frowned. "You look displeased, Miss Parker. Don't worry. We'll always be friends, whether I stay here or go elsewhere."

"I am well aware that we will always remain friends, Miss Grant," Vicky replied in a clipped tone. "But it is the advice and friendship I receive by merely walking next door that I will miss. Waiting for a reply to a letter will take far too long."

"I see," Laura said with mock indignation. "Is that the only reason you are here today? You seek advice?"

Vicky laughed. "No. I needed a break from…well, everything. Work, James's Aunt, and Percy and his inability to understand that he cannot open a frog and insect museum in the office." She gave a pleased sigh. "Life is busy, but it is also quite good."

"Is the aspiring gossip columnist still prying into your business?" Laura asked with a grin. It was a very good way to describe Miriam.

Vicky nodded and explained what had taken place during their last two outings. And as she had not spoken to Laura since, she included her earlier argument with James. "I must admit, I doubt we have had such a vehement discussion in all the time we have known one another, and I am uncertain how to feel about it."

"Disagreements are inevitable," Laura replied. "What matters are the resolutions that come once they are finished."

With a sigh, Vicky said, "I came over here to get my mind off my troubles. Let us discuss something else. Have you decided what you will do with the offer Richard has made?"

Laura shook her head. "He is everything a woman should avoid but…" Her words trailed off, and Vicky groaned. Was all lost? "What? Can I not think a man handsome?"

"Of course you may," Vicky replied. "Any man but Richard Kent. Oh, very well. You are entitled to do whatever you wish but do be careful. That man is dangerous."

"Speaking of Richard, he said you warned him about the loan he offered me. Thank you."

"Of course," Vicky replied. "I find it odd that he respects my opinion. It makes little sense, really. I mean, who am I that someone such as he should heed me? After all, he does what he wants when he wants, without thought for the outcome." She shrugged. "Perhaps he enjoys the pretense of it all."

Laura chuckled. "He is quite mysterious. Oh, and speaking of mysteries, have you learned anything new about your little inquest?"

Little inquest, indeed!

Vicky explained all she had learned thus far, including her interview with the vicar and Mr. Galpin and what she learned from Mr. Dunne. "I find it odd that her brother would pay men to call on her. It seems a bit…callous in my opinion."

"I remember many years ago when I first opened the shop, he accompanied his mother and sister here to purchase new hats. Even then, long before he'd been given the responsibilities of the barony, he was stern-faced. But he was also sulky. While Miss Gerard looked through the plates, he stood in a corner with his arms crossed over his chest and a scowl on his face. I think he was jealous of his sister receiving a new hat."

"I would not doubt it," Vicky replied. "I wonder if he knew back then about the treasure. Mary Margaret did not learn its location until their father was dying, so he could not have been angry with her about that."

Laura frowned. "Don't tell me you believe all that about a hidden treasure now, too! I thought you were more intelligent than that. Only fools spend their days searching for buried wealth that is not rightfully theirs. If I had a farthing for every story I've heard about a missing treasure, I'd not need to keep my shop open."

"I did not believe it at first, but now I am beginning to do so. What man would go to such lengths to learn its location if it did not exist?"

Laura shook her head and sighed. "Oh, you may be right; perhaps this particular tale is true. But if it is, and you learn the truth about it, will you tell Lord Gerard?"

"That was our agreement," Vicky replied. "And I keep my promises. Plus, I care nothing for the treasure. I only agreed to this inquest to secure a place for Percy at Eton School. After all, who could pass up such a wonderful opportunity?" She sighed. "The problem is that I have seen what wealth can do to people. I hope the baron does not renege on his promise once he has the information he has been searching for. Regardless, I will hold up my end of the bargain. If he does not, he will be the one to carry the knowledge that he cannot be trusted. I will retain my integrity."

Thankfully, the conversation turned to other, less oppressive matters, and soon, Vicky was ready to return home. Mr. Dunne had gone, but she could hear Mr. Thompson in the new office area. And Percy.

"This's me favorite rock," Percy was saying. "'Is name's Ralph. If ye need yer work done, 'e'll do it fer a 'ole week for jus' a shillin'. Ye can pay me if ye wan'."

Mr. Thompson chuckled. "I am unsure if Mr. Kensington would approve of that arrangement, young man, but I will certainly consider it."

Vicky smiled and walked into the room. "Percy, Mr. Thompson has work to complete. We spoke about this yesterday, remember? You are not to bother him while he is working."

Percy's shoulders slumped. "I know, but I wanted someone to play with me. Everyone's so busy." He stopped and smiled. "Will ye play with me?"

The idea of playing with rocks was not very appealing but spending time with Percy was a good use of an afternoon. "I would love nothing more," she replied.

Chapter Sixteen

Vicky held Percy's hand as she walked with James and Miriam past the houses located close to Regent Street. Miriam had insisted they spend the morning surveying the homes, allowing her the opportunity to give her opinion on what life would be like for them if they were to live there. The homes were elegant, especially when compared to the living quarters available above many of the shops on Wellington Street. They had steeply sloped roofs and ivy crawled up the facades of many of them, and although they did not have as many bays as the houses located on Grosvenor Square, it did not make them any less impressive.

As far as Vicky was concerned, she was not moving houses anytime soon, nor did she plan to leave the area around Wellington Street, but what harm was there in admiring these homes? Not only did it please Miriam, but James also seemed to be enjoying himself, as well.

Plus, according to the information Lord Gerard had given her, Mr. Christopher Haring lived not two streets away.

"Just think of the parties you will be able to host," Miriam was saying to James, who had offered her his arm. "Your guest list could begin with your friends and clients, but as word travels about the success of the firm, more members of the *ton* will avail of your services."

James was grinning from ear to ear. "I would like that very much," he said. "Though, if I were to be honest, these homes are far too expensive. I doubt I will ever receive an income that will allow us to make such a hefty purchase. I would hate to see us thrown out on the streets when we are unable to pay the terms of a mortgage!"

Miriam came to a stop and placed a hand on James's arm. "Once one comes to market, I will give you enough money to pay toward the balance so the payments are more than manageable. I would only ask for one thing in return."

"And what is that?" James asked.

Vicky held her breath. Whatever this woman requested would likely be more than she cared to pay.

"I...No, I cannot make such a request," Miriam replied with a sigh. "Forget I said anything. The rooms at the Royal Mayfair are adequate, though small and a bit drafty. Asking to stay with you if I was to visit would be asking far too much."

"If you wish to stay with us once we are married," James said, his smile never faltering, "the answer is yes. We should have more than enough space to choose a room that is dedicated just to you, one no one else will use. Is that not right, Victoria?"

Vicky swallowed hard. "I see no reason to reject such a plan—"

Miriam gasped. "Are you saying that if I plan to visit for several months, you will not mind if I stay with you? Oh, James, tell me you are not teasing me!"

James laughed as they continued their stroll. "You are family, Aunt Miriam, and my home shall be your home. Whether it be for a week or many months, you may come and stay as long as you wish."

The thought of Miriam being with them in the same house for an extended period of time filled Vicky with terror. Being in her company for a few hours several days a week was difficult enough; what sort of torture would life be like with this woman living in her home?

"And when your first child is born," Miriam continued, "I will remain for the first year. After all, every young mother can benefit from instruction on how to raise a child properly."

Vicky nearly bit her tongue in two to keep from commenting.

They stopped before a house with an all-white façade and three steps leading to a portico. A short wrought iron fence sectioned off what appeared to be a lower-level servants' entrance.

Vicky stifled a giggle. What if she went to the wrong house and attempted to enter it rather than her own? After all, every house looked like every other on the street.

Miriam flipped open the fan that hung from her wrist and fanned her face. "It is terribly hot today," she complained.

"Well," James said, "we will be sure your room has a window large enough to allow a cool breeze during the summer and a fireplace big enough to warm you in the winter."

Vicky fumed. They had yet to discuss the possibility of marriage, even though it was likely to happen. And not once had James consulted her on any of the decisions he and his aunt were making concerning *her* future!

She was riddled with guilt for her anger when he turned and smiled at her. "I only want to see that Vicky has everything she deserves," he said. "She has gone far too long without the best things in life, and I plan to right that wrong."

Vicky's heart pounded with adoration. Perhaps she had been hasty in her frustration. What was important in all this was how much she cared for James, and with James came his aunt. She, Vicky, would simply have to learn to make accommodations for a woman who was such an important part of his life. He would have done the same if her mother or father were still alive, she was sure of it.

The bubble of tranquility that had befallen her burst, however, when Miriam said, "Raising children and planning parties requires a great deal of devotion of one's time. Have you considered employing people to be there to help her? She will need a lady's maid, and the children must have a nursemaid and later a governess. Not to mention tutors for any boys you have. And they must not be too pretty. I learned that with Stephen. Too often, pretty women employed in one's residence attempt to seduce the man of the house in order to convince him to give them special privileges. Even while working you are not safe from the wiles of some women."

James laughed. "I am sure I will be fine, Aunt Miriam. I am not so easily seduced."

Miriam sniffed. "Nonetheless, Victoria cannot leave it to chance." She pursed her lips in thought and then added, "I believe I can be of help in that area. Allow me to interview the candidates for those positions."

"If you believe it best," James said with a shrug.

Vicky, however, had heard enough. "Forgive my interruption," she said. "I see there is a park across the way. Perhaps I should take Percy there so he may play for a while."

"Are you trying to avoid spending time with me, Victoria?" Miriam asked. Her smile did not reach her eyes.

"Not at all," Vicky replied. "But as the discussion of my future home and staff seem to be out of my hands, I thought I would leave the two of you alone to make those decisions. Percy, come with me, please."

She ignored Miriam's shocked expression and marched over to a section of grass that housed no more than a few benches beside small flowerbeds. It was far smaller than Ashbey Park, which surprised Vicky. One would have expected a far larger and grander communal area in this part of London. Then again, if the absence of people was any indication, few of the residents spent time here.

"Miss Vicky?" Percy asked as he glanced up at her. "Are ye and Mr. James gettin' married?"

Vicky sighed. "We have not discussed it as of yet, but there is a distinct possibility. What would you think about us marrying?"

His lips twisted in thought. "I think you should," he replied after several moments. "That way ye can ask the rabbit to bring me a brother or sister."

"The rabbit?" Vicky asked, coming to a stop in front of one of the benches. "What rabbit?"

"Ye know. Me mum said that 'tis a rabbit that brings the babies to their mums. The mums write the rabbit an' 'e brings the babies." He tossed one of his rocks from one hand to the other. "I asked 'er why she didn't ask for more babies, and she said it was 'cause she didn't know 'ow to write the letter to ask."

Vicky sat on the bench and smiled. "Well, I most certainly will consider writing a letter, but first I must decide whether or not I should marry Mr. James."

"If ye marry 'im, will that make me yer son?"

Feeling her heart fill with a great warmness, she pulled him in for a hug. "I do not need to be married to consider that. I already think of you as my son."

Percy sighed. "Then don' worry 'bout marryin' 'im then if I'm already yer son."

Vicky laughed until tears ran down her face.

Percy knitted his brows. "Um, can I go play now? I wanna find a new friend for Ralph 'ere." He held up his rock. "But don' worry; it'll be another rock. I know not to bring 'ome any more bugs."

"Yes, of course," Vicky replied. "Go on."

He bounded away, and Vicky could not help but sigh. What she had said was true; Percy was her son now and she the mother he needed. James was like a father to him, but with all that had happened since his aunt arrived, she was unsure if marriage was right for them. Oh, he would make a wonderful husband, but Miriam would be more a mother-in-law than an aunt, and Vicky was unsure if she could stomach her being in their lives as often as she seemed to indicate she wanted to be. What would she do if the woman never left this new home she insisted they purchase?

The concept of marriage was quite different for a spinster than it was for a young lady of marriageable age, Vicky was learning. A spinster lived a far more independent life than her debutante counterpart. Was she willing to give up what she was accustomed to in order to appease a woman who wished to hold the reins of her life?

How did one tell the man she loved these things without hurting him? One way or another, she had to be honest with him; who knew what troubles they would face if she did not! Yet, he adored his aunt, so there had to be something more about her that she, Vicky, was not able to see.

She looked up to see James and Miriam approaching. He smiled as he walked past her and toward the area where Percy was playing.

Miriam sat beside Vicky and patted her hand.

"James is an honorable man," Miriam said. "But like all men, he can be easily lured away by another woman."

Vicky gave her a sidelong glance. "Your husband," she said, choosing her words carefully, "you said he was tempted by other women. Were there many?"

"Oh, yes," Miriam replied in a matter-of-fact tone that surprised Vicky. "Quite a few."

"Please forgive me for asking, but were they mostly maids or did he have some in his business who tempted him?"

"The women at the factory were mostly good, but there was one in particular who smiled at him far more than was proper." She turned to Vicky. "I know you believe I tell you these things to be cruel, but I managed to keep my husband from becoming too attached to any of the strumpets who chased after him. The most important part of being married is to keep your husband happy. If you do not do so, and James decides to have an affair, you will have no one to blame but yourself."

"I do not foresee James ever being unfaithful, and I would prefer not to consider it. Spending all my time worrying about it can only erode away the bliss we would hope to share."

Miriam stood, her lips pursed. "Then enjoy the lonely nights that are certain to come as you wonder where he is and with whom. Do not say that I did not warn you."

James and Percy joined them, and Miriam's tone changed quicker than the weather in an afternoon in the spring. "Ah, there are my two handsome gentlemen. I am sure you will be the talk of the district!"

Vicky sighed when James laughed. She was uncertain what was more stressful, investigating the murder of Mary Margaret Gerard or putting up with Miriam. Well, within a week, neither would be her concern.

Chapter Seventeen

Norfolk Street could have been miles away from Cancellor Street, it was so different. Gone were the elegant facades and front gardens, replaced by bleak, gray-stoned terraced houses in much need of repair. The black trim that once rimmed the windows had peeled away long ago, leaving only tiny remnants that they had been painted at all.

Vicky pulled a piece of parchment from her reticule and unfolded it. Yes, number seventeen was what Lord Gerard had noted beside the name of Mr. Christopher Haring. The house looked even bleaker than its neighbors, if that were possible. A patch of brown on the otherwise blue door said that a knocker had once hung there, but it was no longer present. She rapped her knuckles on the door and waited.

A woman in her late forties with silver streaks in her dark hair and a dress that hung from her skinny frame eyed Vicky with deep suspicion. "Yeah?"

"Good afternoon," Vicky said, offering the woman a polite smile. "Does a Mr. Haring reside here?"

The woman snorted. "'E does 'til Wednesday next, and then 'e'll be finding somewhere else to live. Unless 'e's able to pay his rent, which I doubt'll 'appen seeing as 'e's a week behind and now'll owe me two." She stepped back from the doorway. "Come on in. I'll go fetch 'im for you. 'Less e's dead asleep from the drink." She chuckled at this.

Vicky stepped into the tiny foyer. "Thank you," she said as she surveyed her surroundings. To her right was a doorway that led to what appeared to be a sitting room. In front of her and along the right wall was a staircase that led to the first floor. The entryway was bereft of any sort of décor – no carpets, no paintings, no vases, no figurines of any sort.

"Do I know you?"

Vicky looked up the staircase to find a man in his early thirties peering down at her. He was not a handsome man by any definition of the word, not with his crooked nose that said it had been broken more than once and not properly reset. He staggered as he descended the staircase, and Vicky understood the landlord's concern about the possibility of the man being drunk.

"You don't look familiar, but then my memory's a bit shady at the moment." His shirt appeared to have been slept in and the growth on his jaw said he had not shaved in several days.

"My name is Victoria Parker. Are you Christopher Haring?"

He leaned on the handrail of the stairs. "That's right. And now I'm worried. Why are you here?"

Before Vicky could respond, the woman who had answered her knock stuck her head out a door at the back of the hallway and bellowed, "Dinner'll be at five, you louts! If you're late, you don't eat!" The door flopped to and fro when she pulled back into the room.

Mr. Haring rolled his eyes. "As I'm sure you've figured out, this is a boarding house. Mrs. Doddering has the patience of a squirrel in an oak tree in the autumn when it comes to the dinner schedule. Come in." He led her to the sitting room where several chairs sat in groups of threes and fours, separated by two couches that faced one another. "I'm afraid my monetary situation's at a standstill. Most of my holdings are in…let's just say they are in a state of repair and so I'm forced to live here for a short time. Please, sit."

"I understand," Vicky replied as she sat in one of the chairs, although she doubted he had any holdings of which to speak. "I would like to ask you a few questions concerning the death of a friend of mine, Miss Mary Margaret Gerard?"

Mr. Haring nodded and dropped into the chair across from her, allowing his leg to hang over the arm. "And what is it you're hoping to learn? Mary Margaret and I were close but that doesn't mean I know a whole lot."

"I am curious as to how you and she became acquainted. That would be a good place to begin. Did you meet through a mutual friend, perhaps?"

"A friend?" he asked with a snort. "William Gerard's no one's friend, and I'd know, seeing that we've known one another for many years. But to answer your question, yes, we were introduced by a mutual acquaintance, if that's how you want to look at it. Gerard approached me some time back with an offer. If I wooed his sister and got her to reveal the location of his father's long-lost treasure, he'd share the spoils with me."

"And what was the story he told you?" Vicky asked. "Did he by chance mentioned the value of the missing treasure?"

Mr. Haring nodded. "He did. Well, not an exact value since he himself doesn't know, but it's said that it took many men to carry it."

"When did you first learn about it? Was it when he recruited you for this quest?"

"Oh, no. I heard about the treasure years ago. Lord Gerard, the former, once mentioned it to me during one of his drunken escapades; he said even the greatest financiers could never fathom its worth. I can't tell you how often the son spied on the father only to be caught every time before he could learn where the treasure was located. It became a kind of game to him after a while."

"Did his father ever punish him for his actions?"

Mr. Haring snorted again. "Hardly. The father was far too lenient with the son, and with his ongoing affair, they were always fighting. A few times they even came to blows, and every time they fought, the son would swear that he'd take the treasure from under the old man's nose and leave him a pauper."

"If Lord Gerard, the son, that is, has wanted to learn the location of the treasure so desperately for so long, why did he wait until now to hire men to learn the truth for him?"

"Because he's vain," Mr. Haring replied. "And he's not very intelligent. He's never been able to solve the riddle. He begged Mary Margaret time and again to tell him, even offering to only take a small amount and leave her the majority, but it was her reaction to his last attempt that drove him to search out those of us who were to earn her trust. I suppose you could say we acted as spies for him."

Vicky furrowed her brow. "And what was this reaction that was so different from all those other attempts?"

"She outright laughed. Told him she'd never share the treasure with the likes of someone like him. Or that's what he told me when he came asking me to spy for him."

Interesting, Vicky thought. *Lord Gerard not only acted out of greed, but he also sought revenge for what he likely took as ridicule.* Either made for a strong motive, yet both increased that motive tenfold.

"Will you share with me your account of what occurred the night Miss Gerard was murdered?"

Mr. Haring shrugged. "I see no harm in speaking of that night with you. That earl, Lord Simon Faegan? He'd just left her cottage when I arrived and was heading over to the vicar's place, where Gerard was waiting for him."

Vicky's brows rose. "Was Reverend Lesson there when you arrived?"

"No." Mr. Haring paused, a frown forming on his lips. "Well, yes, I saw him stumbling along near the stables. It was as if the moon were highlighting him, pointing him out. But I didn't care, either way. Mary Margaret looked so beautiful in her blue dress when she answered the door that all thoughts of the vicar, or anyone else, flew out of my mind. And her smile! It was so welcoming. I hadn't seen her so happy the entire time I knew her. It was that smile that had me convinced that it would be me who she told." He sighed heavily. "But alas, it was not meant to be. She served me a glass of wine and then proceeded to tell me that she was no fool, that all along she knew that I'd been putting on a great charade."

"You mean wooing her in order to learn the location of the treasure."

He nodded. "Exactly."

"Was she angry when she made this declaration? Angry that you had tricked her in some way?"

"No, but I responded to her with the same. I said that neither was I a fool, that I'm no child and have no need for friends or romantic entanglements. I left vowing never to return, but before I could reach my horse, I ran into the vicar."

"What was he doing?" Vicky asked.

Mr. Haring chuckled. "The bumbling old codger was singing some ballad in the graveyard next door. He was carrying a shovel over his shoulder, held a lantern in the other hand, and had a length of rope dangling from around his neck. I asked him what he was up to, and do you know how he responded? He said he knew the treasure was buried in the graveyard and that he wanted to start digging right away! He's a bit dicked in the hob in my opinion."

Much of what this man was saying coincided with what Mr. Galpin had said. "And how did you respond?"

"I slapped him," Mr. Haring said. "He should know better; it's blasphemy to dig around on holy ground like that unless he's interring someone. He ran back to his cottage, sobbing like a child who's been beaten by his father for misbehaving." He barked a laugh at that. "Then I left and returned home."

"And did you see or encounter anyone else?"

He shook his head. "Not a soul, and being as I was the last one to see her that night, I already know the constable's going to come after me and accuse me of murdering her. It won't matter that she was alive when I left the place."

"I spoke to a man named Donald Galpin. At the risk of offending you," in all reality, she doubted rather highly that there was any risk in what she was about to say, "but he believes you have the best motive to murder Miss Gerard."

Mr. Haring pointed a grimy finger at her. "That drunken fool dares to accuse me? He was so in love with Mary Margaret that it would've made you sick up. Did you know that he stayed at her cottage overnight on more than one occasion? He said it was all innocent, and I believe him on that matter. Not because I trust his word, mind you, but because Mary Margaret was no loose woman.

But he was so sure he was the one she'd reveal the location of the treasure to that he took out several loans from men who…let's just say they aren't upstanding moneylenders. Now they're calling for his head because he can't pay his debts. Well, good riddance to him, I say!"

He pulled himself from the chair and stood. "Now, I've got to wash up for dinner or Mrs. Doddering'll let me starve, and it doesn't matter meals are supposed to be included as part of the board."

Vicky stood but she had one more question before she left. "The morning after Miss Gerard died, did the baron come to speak to you?"

Mr. Haring scowled. "How'd you know that? Ah, well, it doesn't matter. Yes, he arrived just after sunrise. Woke me from a dead sleep, too."

"May I ask what you discussed?"

"I don't think you'd want to know what he asked me," Mr. Haring said with a deep chuckle. "In fact, I'd say it's prudent you don't ask."

Vicky straightened her back and gave him a pointed look. "Trust me, Mr. Haring, I am certain nothing you say can surprise me."

He shrugged. "Fine. The baron told me Mary Margaret was dead, that she'd been murdered and her body was left to rot in the graveyard. But I think he knew more than what he was saying because he knew things only the murderer could've known. Such as the fact that she was strangled with a rope. I'd say it was him who murdered his sister, which is why I ran off. I figured the blame'd be put on me. But then I realized running only made me look the guilty one, so I thought it best to return and see what happened."

"And why do you believe that Lord Gerard informed you that his sister was murdered? If he is the murderer, why reveal such information so early and so carelessly?"

"I don't know. Maybe because he was drunk or had gone mad. I'd go mad if I'd murdered someone, wouldn't you? I just pray he doesn't remember coming here, that it was someone else who told you about his calling on me, or you'll be asking questions about my death next!"

Chapter Eighteen

The tailor's shop owned by Mr. Rightford on Oxford Street was no different from most establishments of its kind. Unlike a dressmaker's, the main area of the shop had nothing more than a short counter beside one wall and a few displays of the various accessories a man might purchase to accent the coats and other important clothing the tailor created for him. Men had little need for the rolls of ribbons and grand boards of swatches displaying the choices in fabric colors and prints women so desired.

Vicky found it strange that Lord Gerard had asked that she leave a message with Mr. Rightford, but if this was how he preferred she contact him, she had little choice but to do as he asked.

"My apologies, Miss Parker," Mr. Rightford said. He was a thin, balding man with tiny round spectacles that sat on the tip of his nose. His hands fidgeted as if he had not given up his stitching despite the fact he held no needle. "Lord Gerard is away on business and is not due to return for several days, and he gave me no indication as to how long he will be gone. If you would like, I can send a runner to inform you when he has returned. I have every confidence that he will call as soon as he is in London."

That had been three days ago.

In order to keep busy, Vicky focused on her work and schooling Percy. Between the two, she had little time to breathe. Laura had left to Folkestone just as she said she would, and James spent most of his evenings with his aunt. It was a relief that Miriam had not insisted she join them for whatever form of entertainment the woman had chosen.

Once Percy was put to bed, she was given the opportunity to think. Many of her thoughts were on the future and the likelihood of spending it with James as her husband. She had little doubt that he would soon propose, and she had no reason to refuse.

Yet, one concern continued to assail her – the several conversations they had shared recently that focused on material things. Too many men who relied upon Parker Accounting office had spent themselves into bankruptcy, and she could not allow the same to happen to them because James chose to follow his aunt's suggestions.

She looked up at the clock on the mantle. The office would officially close in a few minutes. She had sent Mr. Thompson home early, and James had left an hour earlier, although he did not explain where he was going. Likely to meet his aunt, if Vicky were to hazard a guess.

Please do not bring Miriam here, she prayed silently.

For a moment, a pang of guilt touched her, but she pushed it aside. Miriam would be gone in one more week, and peace would be restored to her life. If luck was with her, Miriam would wait to return until the wedding. A bit of reprieve before she moved in with them would be nice, but perhaps they should discuss expectations before that happened.

Making a final notation in the ledger on which she was working, Vicky set it aside to dry and replaced the pen to its holder just as the front door flew open.

"Victoria," James said as he hurried into the room, "I have the most wonderful news!"

Annoyance coursed through her. "I really do wish you would not insist on calling me Victoria. You know very well I prefer Vicky. At least from you."

He smiled. "Oh, very well," he said, undaunted. "I will use Vicky when my aunt is not with us."

He had missed the point completely, but it was a start. "Thank you," she replied. "Now, what is this news you wish to share? Have you secured us yet another account?"

James shook his head, his boyish grin melting her heart. "I spoke to Aunt Miriam about the lessons she wanted you to have, and I told her in no uncertain terms that you did not need them."

A sense of pride and gratitude washed over Vicky. He had championed for her! Her love for him deepened, and she threw her arms around him and laid her head against his chest.

"Thank you," she said. "This means so much to me, more than you could ever know."

"I am glad," he said with a laugh. "But that is not the best news."

She pushed away from him. "Oh?" she said, her voice trembling. "And what is this 'best news'?"

"I purchased a horse for you!" he replied. "And not just any horse; a horse worthy of flaunting before everyone! It will cost a pretty penny, but it is worth it. You will be the envy of all our friends!"

She stared at him. Had he gone mad? "Please tell me you are jesting," she said. Her heart sank when he shook his head. "James, I have no experience with riding; there has never been a need here. Plus, we have nowhere to keep such an animal."

"That has been decided already," he replied. "I found a man who can stable it for us and all you need to do is go there whenever you wish to ride. They will provide everything – stabling, feeding, brushing...whatever it takes to care for a horse. You will not have to worry yourself about its upkeep in any way!" He shook his head in wonderment. "What a marvelous way to display our wealth."

Vicky frowned. "Display our wealth?"

"Well, yes. Once we are married, the parties we host will allow us to make new friends, affluent friends. Aunt Miriam said that owning a horse was just one type of luxury that will make us stand out from our peers all the more."

Vicky was finding difficulty in making sense of his words. It was as if her head were filled with cotton wool. "Parties?"

"Indeed!" he replied with a laugh. "Think of the people who will attend, and believe me, many will wish to attend once they have heard how extravagant they will be. I will be honest; the cost will be extreme at first, but if we are to make the proper impression on the *ton*, we must spend money. It will be well worth it when our guests see the fine food and drink we serve, which will in turn have others vying for invitations to our next parties. Once they are there, I will speak to them about securing their accounts."

He grabbed her by the hands and spun her about. "And the wealth, Vicky! Our coffers will grow to overflowing, and we will be happy!"

Who was this man before her? And where had gone the James she knew, the kind, generous, and humble man who had organized a picnic on the floor of the sitting room because the rain had made it impossible for them to be outside?

She did not want to hurt him, but this madness could not continue. "But I am happy now," she said. "We do not need a large house or fancy dresses or even a horse. We only need each other; that is plenty."

He straightened his back and his face took on a stony expression. "Are you saying you do not accept my gift?"

Vicky smiled up at him. "We have love for one another, and that is all I want or will ever need." The disappointment in his eyes made her heart hurt. "If you wish to purchase me a new hat or a dress, I will accept it, for it is something I can use. But a horse? I admit the thought is generous, but we cannot afford something so extravagant."

"I see," James said in an even tone. "Are you asking that I cancel the purchase, then?" He shook his head. "I do not understand the resistance to me buying you a gift. If we are to build wealth together, why must we save it all? I do not want to become a miser, living in squalor because I am too frightened to enjoy the fruits of our labor."

Vicky was growing frustrated in his inability to see the dangerous path he was taking. They were accountants! If anyone knew the importance of keeping a tight rein on spending, it was they!

A knock came to the door, and Vicky sighed. When she opened it, a man grinned around an armful of packages.

"Miss Parker is it?" he asked.

"Yes, I am Miss Parker."

"I've your purchases from Madame Beauchêne's shop," he said. "Would you like me to bring them in for you?"

Vicky had forgotten about the dresses she had ordered the previous week. She had not expected to receive all three at once, and so soon.

"There will be no need," James said from behind her. "I will take them." He gathered the packages and took them upstairs as Vicky placed a silver coin in the hand of the man who had delivered them.

"Thank you, miss," he said with a grin as he lifted his cap and bowed.

Vicky peeked into the kitchen to check on Percy, who was working on his reading. She had made a list of words for him to practice, and he sat hunched over the table, his head tilted to one side as his mouth made exaggerated movements with each sound.

"You are doing wonderfully," she said. He looked up at her. "Are you ready to stop for the day?"

He drooped in the chair and sighed. "I am. Me 'ead 'urts from all this thinkin'."

Vicky laughed. "Why do you not get cleaned up for dinner? You can play with your rocks until it is ready."

With a quick hug, he clomped up the stairs. "Hi, Mr. James," he said as James passed him on the stairwell.

James ruffled the boy's hair and then joined Vicky. "Tomorrow you will be having tea with Aunt Miriam and her friends. You do remember, do you not?"

She had considered every excuse to *not* attend this tea, but none were strong enough to be believable. Perhaps she could indulge the woman this once. After all, she had been able to evade most of the activities planned.

"Of course I remember," Vicky replied with a smile. She turned to face him. "James, I want you to know—"

"Let me ask but one favor," he interrupted. "In a few days, allow me to take you to visit the stable and show you the horse. If you still do not want it, I will not purchase it."

"Will it make you happy if I go?" she asked.

He nodded. "It will. And will you don one of your new dresses? I would like to feel important by wearing our best clothes."

Vicky placed a loving hand on his cheek. "You are important. To me. However, if you wish me to go, I will wear one of my dresses without argument. I just ask that you do not expect me to accept simply because I am willing to accompany you."

"I can agree to those terms," he said. "Wait until you see this animal! It is the finest horseflesh money can buy. You will find yourself unable to refuse it."

With a sigh, Vicky forced a smile. Once she proved to him that they did not need to make such an unnecessary purchase, she hoped their lives would once again return to what it had been when they fell in love.

Chapter Nineteen

As Vicky held one of the three dresses that had been delivered the previous evening, her temper came close to a boil. Wishing to look at the purchases in the natural light of day had made her wait until the morning, but now she wanted nothing more than to return them to their packages and take them out of her sight.

She lifted one by the shoulders and studied it. It was a lovely dark-blue silk day dress covered in white lace – and not what she expected. Nor what she had ordered. Her mind returned to the prior week and Miriam's kind words. Oh, how easily she had been fooled by the termagant! What was meant to build a kinship had become the beginning of the end. Since her arrival, Miriam had charged into Vicky's life like a lioness battling for control. Well, she would never win it if Vicky had anything to do with it!

Then a thought occurred to her. Perhaps it was about time James saw the truth about his aunt. And the dress she currently held might just be what was needed to have that happen.

It was a struggle to balance her anger with sensibility as she considered her plan. If she were not careful, she could hurt James, and that would be far worse than enduring Miriam's attempts at manipulation. Yet, he was blinded by the woman's ability to hide how she responded to those unwilling to fall at her feet.

Perhaps he simply does not want to see…

The thought rang in her head. Miriam was one of the few living relatives James had, not including his brother, Benjamin, and niece, Dinah.

There had been word about some distant cousins in America, but he had never met let alone had a relationship with them.

As wonderful and kind as James was, the once soft-spoken, shy man had finally come into his own in recent months only to retreat back into his old ways so as not to upset his aunt. Or he acted the fool by hoping to brandish wealth he did not possess before people who would never accept him. It made little difference whether or not he had as much as, or more than, those of the nobility. And why? For the simple fact he had no title. And likely never would.

Well, the time has come to set things right!

She draped the dress over an arm and marched out of her room. The office would be closed for another hour but she had heard James and Miriam arrive not long ago. Percy sat between the two adults and it sounded as if Miriam had been telling him a story.

"And that is why you must always address me as Aunt Miriam," she said. "People will ask questions if you do not. Do you understand? We cannot have people gossiping about you."

Percy nodded. "I understand, Aunt Miriam," he said. "An' if anyone asks, I'll tell 'em yer me fav'rite aunt."

Miriam's smile widened. "The boy is wonderful!" she exclaimed. "He will likely become an even better man, perhaps even more so than you, James."

"I will make sure of it," James replied.

Vicky narrowed her eyes at the scene before her. She would never allow this woman to get her claws into another young innocent boy! "Percy, please go to your room and play. I believe I heard Ralph speaking of some sort of adventure, and I would hate to see him sneak away."

Miriam gave Vicky a disapproving look. "Victoria, dear, I have not yet finished speaking to the boy." Her frown deepened. "And why have you not dressed for our outing? I would recommend you go upstairs this instant and change or we will be late. You would not want to embarrass us, would you?" She laughed and turned to James. "I assume you still remember the importance of punctuality, do you not?"

"Percy," Vicky repeated, firmer this time. Miriam clicked her tongue, but the boy nodded and hurried past Vicky. When his footsteps could no longer be heard on the stairs, Vicky rounded on Miriam.

"You lied to me."

James leaped from his chair. "Now, Victoria—"

Vicky tightened her jaw but ignored his attempt to stop her from speaking her mind. "I was told to select three dresses and the fabrics I preferred for each, which I did. Although your aunt suggested some, ultimately, she said the decision was mine."

His brow knitted. "Then what has upset you? You carry one of the dresses now."

"This is not the dress I ordered," Vicky replied. "Now I realize I was duped! While I was sent off to be measured, your aunt changed the order! I may as well not have been there."

James placed a calming hand on her arm. "I am sure it was just a simple misunderstanding. Perhaps the dressmaker became confused. If you do not like the dress, I am sure that can be remedied. Am I not correct, Aunt Miriam?"

Drawing a much-needed calming breath, Vicky turned her attention to his aunt. "Why did you change my order? I specifically told you I was uncomfortable with this style. Do you wish to control me as you control James?" The words left her lips before she could stop them.

Miriam rose from her chair and let out an exaggerated sigh. "James, it is important that you know Victoria is telling the truth. There was no misunderstanding."

"No misunderstanding?" James asked. "But how…?"

"When Victoria expressed her displeasure at my choices, it saddened me. I admit that I betrayed her by returning to Madame Beauchêne and changing the order without her knowledge."

Vicky stared at Miriam. She had not expected an outright admission of guilt. Was this an attempt at apologizing for her betrayal? Perhaps she, Vicky, had been too quick to judge the woman's motives.

"It is as if I do not know you," James said, his voice forlorn. "Why would you do such a thing? This is so unlike you."

Miriam gave a sad nod. "That day at the dressmaker's, I saw not only our bride-to-be but a woman unaware of how lovely she truly is. When I made my suggestions, I could see her fear of a style so different from what she is accustomed to wearing."

Her gazed dropped to the floor. "I thought...no, I did not think. I simply wanted her to look so beautiful that all of London would talk of her."

For a moment, Vicky's heart constricted. Had she been too quick in her accusation? Yet when Miriam peeked up at them, an image of a willful child appeared in Vicky's mind, for Percy had done the same on many occasions as a way to avoid punishment. The woman meant none of what she said!

"Now I realize that, once again, my good intentions and desire to lend my aid are unwelcome." She raised her face and looked at Vicky. "Forgive me. I only wanted to help."

James gave Vicky no chance to respond. "There is nothing to forgive. As I suspected, you meant no harm. However, I must ask that you not do something like this again."

"I promise I will not," Miriam replied. "I will reimburse you the cost of the dresses since you do not want them. It is a waste, but it is merely money, after all."

Thus far in her life, Vicky had met some nefarious people, yet Miriam was as crafty as any of them. Even Richard Kent acted more an adult than this woman!

James, however, did not see his aunt's deviousness. "You would not mind wearing that dress today, would you, Victoria? It would make Aunt Miriam happy if you did and you will not have to wear it again if you choose not to do so."

Vicky had to take a breath to calm the urge to throw the garment on the floor and stomp on it. The last thing she needed to do was act as childish as his aunt. "Will you excuse us, Miriam?" she asked. "I would like a word alone with James." Without waiting for a response, she turned on her heel and marched into the office.

"Victoria?"

She blinked back the tears of anger that threatened to spill over her lashes. She despised this problem being forced between them. "I will make you a promise," she said finally, turning to face him. "If you wish me to wear this dress, I will. However, after today, I have the right to refuse any outing with your aunt. And she is not to fill Percy's head with ideas, either."

James's face darkened, and Vicky could not stop a tear from trickling down her cheek. "You do not see it, do you? Miriam seeks to control me as she does you, but nothing I say or do seems to make you understand the truth."

"You do not know her," he said, his voice tight with anger. "She does not control me, I can assure you. She has a good and pure heart, and yes, she does tend to fight to get her way, but only to better a person."

"Be that as it may, that is my request. And once she is gone, we must have a discussion concerning us."

"Why wait?" he demanded. "Why not discuss your concerns now?"

"Very well," she replied, straightening her back. "Decisions about dresses," she lifted her arm to show the one draped over it, "horses, homes, children, everything that you have discussed with her should be reserved for us. No one else should have a say in what we decide for our lives."

He looked down at her, his jaw tight. "Very well, then. You have made it perfectly clear that any attempts to better our life is your decision and yours alone. I will no longer argue with you about it. Forgive me for wanting to place you in a position that will see you among the finest ladies in London."

"I am already the best woman I can be. Not because of the clothing I wear or the horses I own, but because I have you. Because I love you."

He shook his head and gathered her into his arms. "And I love you. I did not mean to hurt you, and for that I am sorry. My aunt will be gone in less than a week. Can you please not simply make the attempt? For me?" He lowered his voice. "I know she can be a little overbearing."

A little?

"But I do love her," he continued. "It is important to me that she feels welcome."

Vicky sighed. "Very well, I will wear the dress today for the tea party. But make no mistake, I do it for you and for no other reason. Is that clear?"

He smiled down at her. "Thank you. Trust me, you will see. Aunt Miriam means well and is only looking out for us."

"Now, you I trust," she said with a playful laugh. "And I had best change if I am to get this over with."

Once in her room, she donned the new dress, refusing to ask Miriam for help with the stays. It took her longer than it typically would have, but when she was finished, she looked herself over in the mirror. Her cheeks were red with embarrassment. Never had she worn a garment with such a revealing neckline!

When she met Miriam in the vestibule, Vicky was grateful for the shawl the woman placed over her shoulders. If she was lucky, there would be no reason to remove it.

"I know you do not want me in your life," Miriam said, "but you will see that I only wish to help. Today you will meet ladies of good standing. Let us just say that the connections you make at this gathering will set you up for the rest of your life."

Vicky pursed her lips before turning to give the woman a tight smile. "You sound as if you are describing yourself, but I know you would never be so vain as to say as much."

Miriam laughed, clearly missing the bite of Vicky's words. "You are correct; I am not. Now, come. Let us go before we are late and make a bad impression.

Chapter Twenty

The home of Lady Joanna Barton was a five-minute ride from Wellington Street. Vicky and Miriam were ushered into the parlor as if they had arrived late to an important event, though the bells rang one, the scheduled time of the tea, as they knocked on the door.

Three women of varying ages sat on a long couch and another stood beside the fireplace.

"I have no doubt Lord Chelmsford has more bastard children than I own dresses," the woman standing said with a sniff. She was in her mid-fifties with faint lines in the corners of her eyes. Her green dress had an overlay of intricate white lace and green slippers peeked from beneath its hem. "And to think his wife denies his wrongdoing! One would think the hiring of new maids every nine months would enlighten her." This brought about a few titters from the other women. "And I will resume the story in a moment." She turned to Vicky and Miriam, kissing the latter on each cheek. "I am so pleased you are here, my dear friend. And you brought a guest."

When all eyes turned to Vicky, her face heated.

"It has been far too long, Joanna," Miriam gushed. "May I introduce my soon-to-be niece-in-law, Miss Victoria Parker. Victoria, this is Lady Joanna Barton, Baroness of Chesney."

Vicky bobbed a curtsy. "My lady." She did not miss the whispers between the trio on the couch.

Lady Barton looked her up and down. "My, she is beautiful, Miriam. Your James is a fortunate man, indeed. Please, Victoria, you are amongst friends here. There is no need for formalities. I am simply Joanna when we are together."

"Thank you," Vicky replied. The woman indeed made her feel welcomed.

One of the women from the couch stood. "Since Joanna has thrown out all sense of politeness," she said, although her tone was more playful than admonishing, "allow me to introduce myself. I am Lady Grace Spalding, Viscountess of Talberton – but just Grace, mind you. The young lady with the lovely auburn locks is Miss Phoebe Nance, and the other young lady at the end is Miss Eliza Barton, Joanna's niece."

Vicky studied the women. Grace, who appeared in her mid-thirties, had blond hair styled into a perfect chignon with two long curls framing her doll-like features. Phoebe was closer to Vicky in age and had the most vivid green eyes she had ever seen that complimented her fiery red hair. Eliza had her aunt's dark hair, but where Joanna's eyes were blue, Eliza's were chestnut.

"Come, Victoria," Miriam said as she made her way to a smaller sofa. "Sit beside me."

Joanna resumed her discussion of Lord Chelmsworth. "As I was saying, Phyllis is oblivious to what her husband is doing."

The door opened and the butler entered, a silver tray ladened with a teapot, teacups, and a plate of tiny cakes and tarts in his hand.

As he poured, Joanna continued. "Yet her dismissal of her husband's dalliances has nothing to do with ignorance or a refusal to admit to the truth." She leaned forward, her eyes twinkling mischievously. "I understand that she and her butler have had a number of indiscretions!"

The ladies giggled, but the butler's eyes widened before he schooled his features once more. He hurried his task, gave a swift bow, and left the room, a blush spreading across his face.

Eliza sighed. "His son is not any better, you know."

Miriam clicked her tongue. "I could not agree with you more."

"Why do you say that?" Phoebe asked.

"Because just last week, he propositioned me!"

"Oh, Eliza," Miriam said, "the shame of the man! What did he say?"

Eliza blushed. "He admired my dress and asked me where I had purchased it so he could have one ordered for his wife, but we know that such innocent talk is only a masquerade for desire. Thankfully he said this in a ballroom full of witnesses. If he had caught me alone, who knows what he would have done!"

Vicky could only stare as the ladies continued their gossip, each sharing more absurd stories than the one before it, all without a shred of evidence that those they discussed had done anything wrong. Was this how women of the nobility spent their time, speaking falsehoods about their peers? If so, she wanted nothing to do with it.

Grace glanced around at the group. "I was kissed by a rogue."

A collective gasp filled the room.

"Please tell me that nothing else occurred," Joanna said.

Grace shook her head. "I was able to fight him off," she said as she rose and walked to the fireplace. Vicky had determined that if a woman was about to tell a story of substance, the fireplace was where it would take place. "My Evan and I hosted a party, a small gathering where he and his friends could play games of chance. Among them was Mr. Richard Kent. He actually grabbed me, threw me against a wall, and kissed me!"

"What did you do?" Eliza asked, her eyes sparkling.

"I admit I was stunned," Grace replied. "He told me he had never seen a woman with my beauty and could not restrain himself. I warned him to never do it again or I would tell Evan, and I assure you, he will call out Mr. Kent to duel if he were to learn of his forwardness."

Of all the shocking things Vicky knew of Richard, forcing a kiss from a woman was not one she would have considered. Oh, a rogue he was, to be sure, but he likely had plenty of amenable women to play his games; what need did he have to assault one who was unwilling?

Grace continued with a deep sigh. "Even in my own home I struggle to keep men at bay." She went on to accuse the baker, a footman, and even a cousin of being too forward with her, insisting that she was lovelier than any other woman they had seen, or other similar comments. "Beauty is a heavy burden to bear," she said as she returned to her seat.

Joanna turned to Vicky. "And you, Victoria. How is it that you met Miriam's nephew? Was it at a party?"

Vicky smiled, relieved her story would be far different from those these women told. It was a true romance that spoke of a young hero coming to her rescue just when she needed him most.

Before she could share her story, however, Miriam spoke up. "Victoria's father owned the accounting firm when James was hired. Sadly, he died, leaving Victoria to take the reins of the firm." She gave a sniff to express what she thought of that. "She could have easily drowned in her sorrows, but she held firm to her belief that Parker Accounting would remain profitable. Which is why she asked James to take her father's place as head of the firm." She patted Vicky's hand. "The poor thing had no idea what to do, and she had many unscrupulous men vying for her hand just so they could gain control of the business."

Eliza clicked her tongue in vexation. "So many men have no sense of decency."

"I could not agree with you more," Grace said with a firm nod. "We are nothing more than fresh meat to be devoured by some of them. Thankfully, none have succeeded in their pursuits of me."

Miriam cleared her throat, and the women fell silent. "As I was saying, my nephew not only saved her failing business, but he also made it more profitable than it had been before Mr. Parker's passing. Victoria was close to losing everything, but I am pleased to say that those days are far behind them because of what James has been able to do."

Joanna heaved a heavy sigh of admiration. "What a lovely story. To think so many pursued you…well, that no longer matters. I can see how a marriage between you and James will benefit you both. It will be an arranged marriage, will it not?"

Again, Miriam spoke for Vicky. "Not at all! My James has admitted to admiring her beauty after being in the employ of the firm for so long. Thankfully, he had the foresight to not fall for her charms until he saw the firm placed on level ground once again."

This made the others laugh politely, but to Vicky's surprise, Eliza frowned.

"I have heard of Parker Accounting," she said, her brows knitted tightly together. "My husband's cousin, Timothy, has been a client for years, long before Mr. Parker died. According to him, he continued to do business with Miss Parker long after her father's passing, as did many men."

Silence filled the room, and Miriam twisted her lips and said in a harsh whisper, "Do not allow James to look a fool, Victoria!"

Vicky took a deep breath and slowly released it. "James was hired by my father, and upon his death, I indeed asked James to remain and oversee our clients. Although we were not near bankruptcy, he has indeed been an integral part in how it stands now. He has brought in a number of influential clients."

"And what of the men who attempted to woo you?" Joanna asked with great enthusiasm. They were enjoying Vicky's story immensely. "Is that true, as well?"

"It makes little difference now," Miriam said quickly. "Once they are married and James takes control of the firm, he will continue to bring in clients. And, for a wedding gift, I am securing a house for them near Regency Street."

"Oh, how wonderful!" Phoebe said.

"My home is located there," Grace added. "We shall be neighbors! Is that not marvelous?"

"We must host a party here in celebration," Joanna offered. "And Victoria, once you are married, you must agree to join us. We meet twice a week. Oh, and you must attend our parties and we will attend yours. We will have so much fun!"

Vicky smiled and nodded, pretending to be interested as the women continued to talk. How strange it all was! Why would any of these women be interested in her, a lowly accountant?

Miriam dominated the conversations with ways she would help her and James to find their way among the upper class.

Then she mentioned Percy. "The child was born to a woman who has no husband, unfortunately. He will need to make drastic changes if he is to be accepted into society. After all, some may find his speech enduring now, but if he continues to act like a common street urchin, he will be ridiculed by all the young boys, those who count, that is. I plan to do what I can to help him reach his potential but living outside of London for now will be of no use to the boy."

Vicky had heard enough. "Percy's acceptance into societal circles should be based on his character, not his speech, a characteristic that can be corrected with instruction. I have plans to see that he receives a proper education, but my hope is to have him possess a sense of morality, integrity, and above all, kindness for others. Those attributes are far more important than any other he could have gained from simply being born into a noble family. No offense to the nobility. I only mean that coming from an aristocratic background does not guarantee decency. Have you not proven this by the stories you have told here? Therefore, I will see that he gets all the help he needs to become the man he is meant to be."

"I could not agree with you more," Joanna said with a serious nod. "Miriam, you may mean well, but this boy is not your child to raise. Victoria does not need your nosing into her affairs, especially with a child that has been placed in her care. Clearly she has the ability to see he has a proper upbringing without input from anyone else, you included. Now, do not be offended, my dear. I only say this because I am your friend."

"Of course, you are right," Miriam replied in such dulcet tones, she would not need sugar in her tea for a week.

The conversation moved to other topics, and Vicky glanced at Miriam, who refused to meet her eyes. They rode back to the office in complete silence, the woman uttering a quiet "Good afternoon" before the carriage pulled away, leaving Vicky staring after it.

"So, how did it go?" James asked. "Did you enjoy yourself?"

Vicky was uncertain how to feel about what had taken place at the tea party. She should have been ecstatic that Miriam was put in her place, but somehow she knew saying so would disappoint James. "I did."

He looked past her. "Did my aunt not wish to see me?"

"It is not that, I am sure. I believe one of her friends may have said something that upset her. When are we to go look at the horses?"

"Tomorrow," James replied. "I received word that Lord Dreadman wishes to come by and speak with me about our services."

"Tomorrow then," Vicky said, feeling a heaviness in her stomach, not for the idea of going to see the horses but also for how James would react when his aunt explained what had actually taken place at the tea. It was not that Vicky had lied, for it was Joanna who had said the words that upset Miriam, but Vicky had initiated the thorn that became embedded in his aunt's side.

As she changed into the dress she had been wearing before their outing, Vicky considered how the day had gone. In a way, it had ended better than she had believed it would, albeit not better for Miriam. Now that James's aunt had heard the truth from a friend, perhaps she would finally step aside and allow James and Vicky to lead their own lives.

Chapter Twenty-One

Wellington Street sat virtually empty as the clock struck eight, the only evidence of life a lone dog nosing from corner to corner, his tongue lolling as he trotted along. Vicky had put Percy to bed an hour earlier – after telling him a story, of course – and the boy was likely already dreaming of searching for more rocks to add to his collection. If he brought any more of his "pets" into the house, Vicky worried the upstairs would fall into the downstairs from the excess weight of all his new "friends".

Vicky was enjoying a glass of wine when a carriage pulled up in front of the office. Lord William Gerard had finally returned to London. Despite the need to speak to him, Vicky was not in the mood to do so tonight. Although Lord Gerard had given his word to honor his end of their strange bargain, she was curious to see if any sort of circumstance arose causing him to change his mind. She would not be surprised if that were to happen, for she had never truly trusted the man.

As Lord Gerard made his way to the door, Vicky went to greet him.

"I only returned to London three hours ago," the baron said, removing his hat and bowing. "I did not wish to wait and send word of my return, so I hope you do not mind too much that I have called so late. I simply cannot wait to hear what you have learned thus far."

"Of course not, my lord," Vicky replied, hoping the man had forgotten his request to not use his title. "Please, come in. Would you care for a glass of wine? Or perhaps I can get you some tea?

I am afraid I have no brandy at the moment."

"No, thank you," the baron said as he undid the button on his coat and sat in one of the two chairs in front of the large desk. "I presume you have learned the location of the treasure?" His eyes gleamed greedily as he asked this. He truly did not care who murdered his sister!

"I am drawing closer to it," Vicky replied. "But I have further inquiries to make, questions that must be answered, before I can say for certainty."

Lord Gerard blew out a breath. "I have changed my mind. I will take a glass of wine."

With a nod, Vicky went to the kitchen and by the time she returned, the baron had lit a candle that sat on the desk although the sun had not yet fully set.

That is rather forward of him, Vicky thought. As if he were the one who purchased the candles for the office!

She handed him the wine, for which he thanked her, and then said, "I wish to ask you about your father, if I may." She ignored the curse the man said under his breath. "What was your relationship like with him before he died? I know you spoke of it briefly, but surely you shared some sort of bond as father and son."

He snorted. "My father and I were oftentimes at odds with one another. There were things that I could simply not accept, and that is all I will say on the matter."

"You have mentioned on several occasions that he spoke often about returning to his treasure to gaze upon it, but he refused to allow you to join him. Is that correct?"

The baron frowned. "I told you all you need to know to solve this mystery. Whether or not his times away were to view his treasure or something else matters little."

Vicky interlaced her fingers on the desk in front of her. "But it does matter, my lord. I must know if this treasure created a rift between you and your father. It is imperative if you wish to know its location."

Lord Gerard sighed and leaned back in his chair. "Indeed, we argued, and often. I knew my father sneaked away to have a look at the treasure, sometimes once a week and other times he would wait an entire month.

I always knew when he had gone because his eyes sparkled upon his return."

"And still, he would not reveal it to you?"

The baron shook his head. "No. He told me I could never share in it, that I was unworthy and would never comprehend its true value. I, the man who would assume responsibility for the barony when he was gone, was unworthy of his greatest wealth! It was preposterous! Mary Margaret, however, was another thing altogether. He always said she would appreciate it more than I."

"And for that reason I must ask, why? Certainly you have some sort of explanation. Was it simply because he favored her over you, or is there more to this story than you are willing to reveal?"

"Perhaps he had intended to use it as a means to see she had a dowry worthy of a duke or a prince, yet she never took advantage of its wealth. She could have married the most eligible bachelor of the *ton*, but she whiled away her years reading and hiding. I have no idea what made her finally decide to marry, and at such an advanced age, but I was not surprised when she used the treasure as a means to attract suitors."

"Yet, you hired men to play those parts," Vicky reminded him.

"Of course I did," he snapped. "I could not have her husband taking possession of what should have belonged to me, my father's heir, in the first place. Providing her suitors allowed me to control who she chose. Everything belonging to the barony, including all wealth, should come to me. If my father believed I would not take care of my sister, he was sadly mistaken. I saw she received her allowance every month. I could have lessened it, given her just enough to cover the bare necessities, but I did not. As a matter of fact, she received ten pounds more per month than our father allotted her, which is much more than a spinster needs to live a comfortable life. Faith! She could have hired a full staff of servants and still had enough money to purchase a new dress every month! Now, enough of this. Have you learned who murdered my sister? More importantly, do you know where I can find the treasure?"

"Not with certainty," Vicky replied. Lord Gerard groaned, but she ignored him. "The night of your sister's murder, I understand that you did not leave immediately. Did you remain to speak to each man after they met with Miss Gerard?"

The baron sighed. "Indeed. And I was forced to endure that fool vicar in between each meeting." He leaned forward and pursed his lips. "What a worthless lout! I sent him to listen outside Mary Margaret's sitting room window so I would know if each man was lying to me when we met afterward, but he was caught. He returned blubbering like an infant, and I had to watch over him like a child as he drank himself into a stupor!"

Vicky sipped her wine to give herself a moment to piece together the baron's story. Indeed, she was drawing closer to the truth and would soon be able to solve the riddle into the murder of Miss Gerard as well as the location of this legendary treasure.

"If you know where I can find it, I will not only see that the boy is given a place at Eton, but I will also share a small percentage of it with you. Say, five percent?"

What Vicky had initially thought of this man, combined with what she had heard, was correct – he was consumed with the legend of this missing treasure. She could not help but feel sorry for him. Men such as he wasted their life searching for what they did not have, missing out on all that life had to offer.

"I will not back out on my promise, my lord. You shall know as soon as I do. I am curious about something, however. The morning following the murder of your sister, you spoke with Mr. Haring, did you not?"

Lord Gerard nodded. "I knew he was the last to see her. I confronted him about her murder, but he denied being the one to kill her." He downed the last of his wine in one gulp and balanced the glass on the arm of the chair. "It was his denial that made me think of you and your insight into such matters. If he was willing to lie outright, then surely others would, as well."

"And you called on him just after sunrise, correct?" The baron nodded. "Did you return home after speaking to him? Or did you happen to go somewhere else?"

The baron narrowed his eyes. "What sort of questions are these? Of course, I returned home after. Surely you do not believe I am complicit in her murder?"

"We made an agreement, my lord, that I would speak to everyone who was there that night. That would include you."

The chair scraped the floor as the baron stood, his face as dark as a thundercloud. "What utter nonsense! Why would I hire you to find my sister's murderer if it was I who killed her?"

"A diversion," Vicky replied calmly. "A way to cast a good light on yourself. Surely such methods are not foreign to you. Have you not done very much the same to your sister for years?"

"But the items I have purchased for her, the talks we had..." His voice trailed off as he lowered himself into the chair and sat in stunned silence for several moments. Then he chuckled. "Ah, very clever, Miss Parker. You have used my own temper against me to catch me in a lie."

Vicky gave him a small smile. "Why would you deny seeing or speaking to your sister that night, my lord?"

"The truth?"

Vicky nodded. "Please."

"Because I believe she is not my sister," he replied. "Or I have my doubts. Do you now understand my anger? I suspect she is the result of my father's affair. He dared to reveal a secret belonging to the Gerard name to a woman whose legitimacy is questionable? If that truth were ever revealed, it would ruin me!"

Schooling her face to hide her surprise, Vicky said, "I am afraid there is no way of knowing if that is true. Did you ever confront your father about this?"

"And risk him disowning me?" Lord Gerard replied, aghast. "Of course not! He already favored her as it was; I certainly did not wish to make matters worse. Now that I have revealed such a shameful truth, what more would you like to know? What other sordid secrets do you hope to learn about my family?"

Vicky did not miss the sarcasm in his tone, which she ignored. She placed the piece of parchment on the desk before her. "On this list are the men you requested I interrogate. What you failed to mention was that you paid them to call on your sister. Why would you lie about that?"

"I did not lie," the baron replied haughtily. "I merely omitted that bit of information. For years, I lavished gifts upon Mary Margaret, begging her to share what she knew. Yet, she chose to embarrass me. You have no idea the number of gentlemen who were confounded by her. She was different from most young ladies on whom they called. For instance, she rejected alcohol of any sort, instead preferring tea at all hours of the day. She refused to engage in normal conversation but instead favored her poetic speech. And this was when she was of marrying age; she worsened as she became older! Those same callers looked upon me with disgust – or even worse, pity – for they believed her to be a lunatic. That was why I hired those men to woo her; I could not chance her losing her mind and never being able to reveal the treasure's location, now could I?" His breath came in heavy gasps when he finished, and Vicky worried he would have some sort of fit.

"You would betray your own sister's heart in order to gain wealth?" Vicky asked incredulously. "Even if you only shared a father?"

"Do not judge me, Miss Parker. If Mary Margaret had simply been honest with me and told me where to find what is rightfully mine, her death could have been avoided."

Vicky studied him for a moment. "And her murderer?" she asked. "What do you believe should happen to him once I have uncovered who he is?"

The baron smirked. "I say he should be tortured until he discloses what he learned, for why would he have murdered her before she revealed the treasure's location unless he wished to keep it for himself? Now, is there anything else you require of me? I am tired after my long journey and would like to go home."

"I have one last question, if I may."

"Go on, then."

"Will you send word that our suspects meet us at the church in three days?"

Lord Gerard nodded as he stood. "I see no issue with that," he replied. "I will see they receive a notice first thing in the morning."

He walked to the door and then stopped to turn back to her. "Do you believe you can get the person who did this terrible deed to reveal the location of the treasure?"

"I do," Vicky replied firmly. "Oh, one last request. Will you also see that a constable joins us at this meeting?"

For a moment, the baron stared at her, but she did not miss the trembling of his hand as he replied, "Yes, of course. I was thinking the same. I shall have a carriage sent to you by ten on Thursday. I assume you will be needing transportation?"

"Thank you, my lord. I will," Vicky replied, pleased she had been able to maintain their somewhat formal standing. Not once did he remind her to use his Christian name, and she was relieved. The last thing she needed was this man seeing her as a close personal friend.

As she closed the door, she sighed. She was certain she had solved the mystery of the missing treasure, and more importantly who murdered Miss Mary Margaret Gerard. That was one area of trouble in her life she could finally put to rest.

Now all she had was the mystery surrounding James and his strange new outlook on what their lives should be like. He had not given up the quest set before him by his aunt, and that worried Vicky far more than finding a killer.

Chapter Twenty-Two

The carriage James had arranged arrived the following morning as promised. With Miriam's help, Vicky had donned her new blue dress once more, not for the sake of his aunt but because James had requested she wear it. Percy also had changed into his suit, and with his cap, he looked the proper little gentleman.

With a shawl wrapped around her shoulders and a hat Laura had gifted her the previous year on her head, Vicky was ready to leave.

"You may close up at noon," Vicky said to Mr. Thompson. "I do not expect any clients while we are gone, but if any arrive before you leave, please record their details and inform them that we will get back to them as soon as we are able." She turned to leave and then stopped with a gasp. "I nearly forgot!" She held up a key by the tips of her fingers. "You will be needing one of your own now."

His eyes were wide. "I will guard it with my life, Miss Parker!" he said. "You can trust that I will see to everything. All will be in perfect order upon your return."

Vicky smiled. "I have no doubt it will. And I believe that with that key come other privileges. I am simply Vicky to my closest friends, so please, address me as such."

With red cheeks, he replied, "T-thank you, Miss...erm, Vicky. And I am Andrew."

"Wonderful! Andrew it is. And I have no doubt that all will be safe in your capable hands." She had to stifle a laugh. She was asking that he simply lock the door when he left, not guard the King's storeroom of gold!

"It is a rare feat for those in accounting," she said, placing the key in the palm of his open hand. Was she terrible for teasing the poor man? Perhaps she was. "You have nothing with which to be concerned, Andrew. You are a highly competent man who is able to lock a door. I have every faith in you. Now, I will see you tomorrow morning."

Andrew nodded as he stared at the key as if it were a most prized possession, but the rigidity of his shoulders had relaxed considerably.

The carriage driver dipped his head and handed Vicky into the carriage. James sat beside Miriam, who offered no smile nor a word of greeting to Vicky.

"Are you ready?" she asked Percy as she sat beside him. "It will be a fun outing."

Percy pulled a white stone speckled with green from his pocket. "I brought Owen," he said with a grin. "'E be a cousin to Ralph and wanted to see the 'orses, too."

"I would leave your rock in the carriage when we arrive at the stables," Miriam said. "We must in no way embarrass Mr. James."

Vicky placed an arm around Percy as the carriage pulled away. Either she confronted Miriam on the absurdity of her comment or she let it go. When she glanced at James, she noted him wringing his hands and decided to remain quiet.

Only a few more days! she thought in a near chant.

"Andrew seemed nervous," James said, giving her a warm smile. "I trust you were able to calm him?"

Vicky laughed. "The poor man acted as if I requested that he guard the office with his life, but I think he was better by the time I left."

"James, dear," Miriam said, placing a hand on his arm, "in the future, it should be you who addresses the help. It will cause less confusion for the poor man, and subsequently the others you employ at a later date. You do not want them to look to Victoria as the one to calm their fears, do you?"

Vicky closed her eyes and said a silent prayer that James would speak up. If he did not, she just might, and the last thing she wanted was to make the day all the more distressing for everyone.

He said nothing, however, and his aunt continued. "What would your mother think of you?" she asked before turning her attention on Vicky. "Linda was always worried about the type of man James would become."

"I believe he has become a dignified and decent man," Vicky said. "I doubt there is any finer gentleman in all of England."

Rather than seeing him encouraged, James stared at the two missing fingers on his hand. For years he had been embarrassed by those missing digits, but in the past few months he had come to accept them as they were. Had his aunt said something to bring attention to them once more?

"Do you truly think she would be proud of me?" he asked in a quiet voice.

"Of course she would," Miriam replied before Vicky could respond. "You have come so far and a grand life lies ahead of you. Can you imagine her being able to witness you hosting a party? Or how proud she would be if she could be with us as you purchase the finest horseflesh in London?"

Sighing, Vicky turned her attention to the passing landscape as they left the town proper. Surely his mother had not been as materialistic as Miriam was implying! From what she had heard, Mrs. Kensington had been a lovely woman everyone respected and many had mourned her death.

The buildings soon became sparse and it was not much later when they turned down a country lane. The carriage wheels hit several ruts in the road, causing them all to bounce about.

Percy laughed with glee as he raised his arms to allow himself to be thrown higher into the air. "Oh, this is brilliant! Aunt Miriam, do ye wanna try?"

"Do not be silly," Miriam replied, grunting when the wheel hit yet another hole. "Ladies and gentleman do not simply jounce about inside a carriage as a form of entertainment."

Vicky pursed her lips. "And as Percy is but a child and not yet a gentleman, I think he should be allowed to find delight in even these small distractions."

Miriam raised her nose in the air and then grasped for the handle above the window beside her, but she did not respond.

The carriage came to a welcome stop, and upon exiting, Vicky looked over the grounds of a small farm. A thatched cottage sat to one side and a stable to the other. A man with a cap much like Percy's approached them, leading a chestnut mare.

"Mr. Martin Robbins," James said to the man, "may I present my aunt, Mrs. Miriam Watson, my fiancée, Victoria Parker, and this young lad is Percy Lock."

It was the first time James had referred to her as his fiancée, and it sent a thrill down Vicky's spine. Perhaps marrying him was what she truly wanted.

"So, Miss Parker," Mr. Robbins said, "I understand she's to belong to you. You're welcome to inspect her if you'd like."

Vicky had little experience with horses, besides those that passed her on the streets, and her hand shook as she reached up to rub the horse's neck.

"She's a mare and quite calm. I'm sure you'll enjoy riding her."

"And she can be stabled here?" Vicky asked.

"Yes, miss. Me and Mr. Kensington've already discussed the cost. You can come visit her whenever you want – even on a Sunday."

"Well?" James asked with clear anticipation. "What do you think?"

"It is a beautiful creature," Vicky replied. "Mr. Robbins, do you mind if I speak to Mr. Kensington alone for a moment?"

"Of course, miss. I'll take her back to her stall. If you want to see her again before you leave, or if you'd like me to saddle her so you can ride, just let me know."

"Come with me, Percy," Miriam said. "Perhaps Mr. Robbins will allow us to look at the other horses."

As the trio walked away, James turned to Vicky. "Well?"

"The horse is magnificent," Vicky replied carefully. "And I can see it drawing the envy of many of the ladies of London if we were to own her. But the truth is I cannot accept such a gift. It is just too much."

"I do not understand," James said. "I can pay for it out of my wages. I am not asking that you give up anything by accepting it. Do you not like horses?"

Vicky sighed. "I like them well enough, but I do not need nor want one." She took his hand in hers. "Tell me the truth. Do you wish to purchase the animal because you believe it will make me happy or do you hope to gain the approval of others?"

The look in his eyes told her that it was indeed the latter, yet James had no time to respond as Percy came running out of the stable, his voice filled with excitement.

"Aunt Miriam says she's gonna buy me a 'orse, too! An' I get to choose it!"

"A young gentleman should learn how to ride," Miriam said as she joined them. "And Mr. Robbins has said that he can provide the animal at a reasonable cost. Now, Percy, which will you choose?"

Vicky took hold of Percy's shoulders. "I am sorry we have wasted your time, Mr. Robbins, but we will not be purchasing any of your horses today. May I offer something for your time?"

"That won't be necessary, miss," Mr. Robbins said. "But I'll be keeping the small deposit Mr. Kensington gave me. He was aware of the risk at the time, I assure you."

Vicky smiled. "I am sure he was. Thank you." As the man walked away, Vicky turned to James. "I will reimburse you—"

James shook his head. "You have embarrassed me enough today," he said in a harsh whisper. "Do not insult me by asking me to take your money." He marched past Vicky and walked over to his aunt, who was dabbing at her eyes.

"I only wanted the boy to have a horse, James," she said. "If Victoria's concern is about the cost of its upkeep, I have the funds to pay it."

Vicky took a hold of Percy's hand. Her head pounded, she was so angry. "It is not about the cost, Miriam, but the motive behind it. I do not want to be the talk of the *ton*, nor the merchants of London for that matter. Furthermore, I have not asked for your guidance concerning our relationship, nor is it needed." She ignored the woman's dramatic moan and pulled Percy to the waiting carriage.

"Miss Vicky?" Percy asked in a small voice. "Are ye angry at me?"

She stopped and squatted beside him. "Of course not," she said, pulling him into her arms. "We simply cannot afford to own a horse, and even if we could, when will we be able to visit it? Do you not think it will get lonely waiting for months before we are able to find a way out here? You have your rocks, and I am sure that is enough."

Percy gave a sad nod, and it took every ounce of Vicky's strength not to turn about and slap Miriam for putting her in this position!

Miriam walked up to them. "The fault is not yours, Percy," she said. "It is I who has angered Victoria. But do not worry, in two days I will say goodbye, and then I shall be out of your life forever."

"But Aunt Miriam," James said as he helped her into the carriage, "that is not what we want…"

Vicky sighed. How could she make James – and Miriam for that matter – see that what they wanted was not what was best for their family? Everything seemed to be falling apart, and she feared that when Miriam left London, James would join her.

Chapter Twenty-Three

The two days following their visit to the stable, James had been unusually quiet. Vicky made every attempt to spark conversation, but he gave only single-word responses or nearly incoherent mutterings. Not only was he distant with her, but he had buried himself in his work, barely taking notice of anything occurring around him.

Vicky thought it best to leave him be for a while. Men could be such sulky creatures sometimes, but they also needed time to puzzle out their problems, much more so than women. Once his aunt was gone, Vicky would sit down with him so they could discuss all that had occurred and thus put their relationship back on the right path.

Miriam had arranged to stop by the office to say goodbye before leaving for home early the following morning. For now, Vicky had other matters to attend to, the most important her meeting at the church in Edgeware. It was time to finally reveal Miss Gerard's murderer. And the location of the legendary treasure.

"Can I wear me 'at, Miss Vicky?" Percy asked as he bounded down the stairs.

He had donned his suit once again, elated he had yet another opportunity to wear what he had deemed his "fancy clothes". Vicky had to admit, he did look adorable in it.

"Yes, you may," Vicky replied. "Are you ready?"

The boy nodded and patted the breast of his suit. "I'm bringin' Ralph with me this time. 'E needs gettin' out once in a while, too."

He glanced past her. "Is Mr. James goin' with us?"

"I am afraid he has a lot of work to finish," Vicky said just as James emerged from Andrew's office.

"You cannot get rid of me that easily, Miss Parker," he said, his usual friendly smile returned. "And I would like to speak to you when we return. The carriage is here, so we must go."

Relief washed over her. The chasm that had come between them had narrowed somewhat, but at least it had narrowed. With a smile, she followed the two men out to the waiting carriage.

She did not recognize the driver who bowed to her. "Miss Parker, I'm to take you to Edgeware."

"Thank you," Vicky said, allowing the man to hand her into the carriage. The benches were plush, unlike the carriage she had taken previously. Was the baron hoping to gain favor by supplying more comfortable transportation than he had previously? Well, she was not easily swayed by such things.

Percy sat beside her and James across.

"When I left school to return to London," James said as he gazed out the window, "I would always ask myself how London could possibly keep changing. I have come to realize that it has never changed." He turned to Vicky. "Oh, new buildings are erected, the fashions change, and there are certainly more people, yet it all remains the same."

Vicky smiled. "Do you believe it will always remain this way?" she asked.

"I do not know but pray that it does."

His answer was as cryptic as his musings could be, and Vicky studied him as they fell silent once more. There was tension around his eyes and he tapped his knee nervously with his left hand. For a moment, Vicky thought over the past two weeks since Miriam's arrival. Was there anything she, Vicky, could have done differently, better choices that she could have made, that would have made his aunt's visit less taxing?

After careful consideration, Vicky concluded that she should have been honest with him from the start. Perhaps they could have avoided all the conflict they had endured.

Well, perhaps when they spoke later, they could clear the air about everything.

The time passed quickly and before she knew it, they came to a stop in front of the church in Edgeware. Two other carriages sat in front of the church building, and two horses had been hobbled nearby. To her surprise, a small crowd had gathered. Word about the revelation of Miss Gerard's murderer had made the rounds.

All the men Vicky had interviewed were present, including Lord Gerard, who was speaking to two men she did not recognize, likely the constable and one of his lackeys.

Lord Gerard hurried toward her. "As you requested, I have invited the constable to join us." He leaned in and lowered his voice. "He is the man wearing a scowl. The other is a Bow Street Runner. I prefer to have London men to take care of London business."

London business? The murder took place in Edgeware. Well, what difference did it make to her?

Vicky's mouth had gone dry. Public speaking, which included any group that went beyond three, was not a pastime to which she looked forward. "And they have agreed to allow me to state my findings?" Vicky asked.

"They have," Lord Gerard replied. "I paid them handsomely for their time. Now, are you ready? The sooner we begin, the sooner I can find my treasure." He rubbed his hands together in anticipation.

"Have everyone gather at the entrance to the graveyard," Vicky said.

The baron grinned. "So, it was there all along, was it?" he whispered. "I thought the vicar was being silly wanting to dig there…Ah, well, never mind." He hurried off to do as she bade.

"Will you be joining me?" Vicky asked James.

"We are," James said as he placed his hands on Percy's shoulders. "I think we will both enjoy hearing what you have to say."

Vicky swallowed hard and made her way around the church to the graveyard. Coming to a stop before the group, she looked at each of the suspects before speaking. "Reverend Lesson, Mr. Haring, Lord Faegan, and Mr. Galpin, you were all hired to woo Miss Mary Margaret Gerard in hopes of learning the location of the Gerard family treasure.

You all did your part to draw her confidence until that fateful night when she invited each of you to call on her. I have concluded that she did indeed reveal the location of the treasure to one of you that night."

"I knew it!" Lord Gerard said. "Speak now, whoever she told, and I may see that your life is spared."

The constable paced before the suspects, halting in front of each one and studying him before moving to the next. Then he stopped before Reverend Lesson. "Do you have a confession to make, Father?" the constable demanded.

"I've done nothing wrong!" the vicar lamented.

Lord Faegan snorted. "The old fool's as crooked as they come. We should march him straight to the gallows. Why bother with a trial?"

The others mumbled their agreement.

Vicky raised her hands to calm everyone. The last thing she needed was for matters to spiral out of control. Yet, no one paid her any mind.

"I say we use the very rope he used on his victim!" someone in the crowd shouted.

"That tree limb there should suffice," said another.

"Quiet, everyone, please," Lord Gerard shouted. "I will not have anyone interrupt Miss Parker again, do you hear?"

A lone bird chirped in the distance as Vicky began to speak. "Lord Gerard was the first to arrive the night of his sister's death. He was angry with her because she had told him that she would never share the treasure with him. After having a glass of wine, he went to the cottage next door, which belongs to Reverend Lesson."

"I open not only the church but my home to any who make a request," the vicar cried.

"Quiet, you!" Mr. Galpin snapped. "Let the woman speak."

Vicky walked over to stand in front of the vicar. "You were the next person to arrive that night, and like Miss Gerard's brother, you, too, drank a glass of wine. I believe she stated that she knew your reason for attempting to woo her. At some point, you confessed that you loved her, did you not? Yet, she did not share your admiration. Am I correct in saying so?"

The vicar nodded. "She said she could never love me."

"You then returned to your cottage, where the baron berated you, correct?"

"There is no need for these trivial details," Lord Gerard snapped. "We have more pressing matters at hand, such as where to find the treasure."

Vicky ignored him. "Lord Simon Faegan, you were next to call on Miss Gerard. However, your conversation was interrupted by a certain vicar who you caught spying on you."

The earl nodded. "That is true."

"It was then that Reverend Lesson went to collect three items: a shovel, a lantern, and a rope."

"Do not attempt to run," the Bow Street Runner said as he placed himself in front of the vicar. "Or it'll be the last thing you do."

Vicky continued. "Then Mr. Donald Galpin arrived and also had a glass of wine. He and Miss Gerard had built a strong friendship, so strong, in fact, that it was not uncommon for Mr. Galpin to stay overnight when it grew too late to travel back to London. You would sleep on her couch so nothing inappropriate took place."

Mr. Galpin dropped his head. "What you say is true. We did become close, but we were never inappropriate in any way; I made sure of that."

"The person who should be cause for more concern above all others is her final guest," Vicky said. "I understand that man was you, Mr. Christopher Haring."

The Bow Street Runner moved behind Mr. Haring, who stared at her with wide eyes.

"You were the last person to see Miss Gerard—"

"No!" Mr. Haring shouted. "I didn't—"

Vicky lifted a hand to interrupt him. "If I were to go by the order of the guest list, you would have been her final guest."

"But what of the treasure?" demanded the baron.

"I am getting to that, my lord," Vicky replied. "Mr. Haring accosted the vicar before he met with Miss Gerard, which led me to realize where the hidden treasure is located. Clearly it is in the graveyard."

Lord Gerard rubbed his hands together. "Brilliant! Now, show me where, so I can begin digging at once."

"Be patient, my lord," Vicky said, a small smile playing on her lips. "I believe we should realize that the person to whom Miss Gerard revealed the secret was not the same man who murdered her."

"What?" the baron barked. "How can that be?"

She swung open the gate. "Follow me, please." She walked down the path that led to the very headstone where Miss Gerard had been found. "When I asked you, Lord Faegan, about your reasons for rejecting the treasure, you responded that you had no use for it. I assumed it was to keep up the pretense of having your financial affairs in order, but that is not true, is it?"

The earl remained silent for several moments before replying, "You are correct. I had to refuse it."

"Reverend Lesson overheard her reveal it to you, which was why he was caught by Mr. Haring with the shovel, the lantern, and the rope. He had gone to collect it before anyone else could."

Everyone turned to stare at the vicar. "I swear I did not murder her!"

"No, you did not," Vicky replied. "But I know who did. You see, I learned that Miss Gerard did not drink alcohol, not even wine, yet five glasses sat on her counter, all empty with only a remnant of wine at the bottom of them. One glass, which had clearly not been drunk, sat on the table. Why would she pour herself a glass if she did not plan to drink it?" She paused. "Because she did not pour it for herself. She poured a second glass for someone who returned once Mr. Haring was gone." She rounded on one of the men. "Did she not, Mr. Galpin?"

"Lies!" Mr. Galpin cried. "I did not return!"

"Neither Mr. Haring nor Reverend Lesson saw you when they were arguing at the gate to the graveyard," Vicky continued. "And when you learned that the vicar knew the location of the treasure, you became enraged. All of your time wasted trying to earn the confidence of Miss Gerard, a spinster in whom you had no true interest, and she dared to reveal her secret to the likes of a vicar? Or so you believed. After all, why else would he be carrying those particular items if not to dig up the treasure? How would he have known that the vicar had merely overheard what had been shared with Lord Faegan?

"So, you, Mr. Galpin, returned, angry and disappointed, to confront Miss Gerard and the two of you argued. It was then that Miss Gerard led you here to explain the truth about the treasure, and in a fit of rage, you strangled her with the rope the vicar had left behind."

"No!" Mr. Galpin wailed as the Bow Street Runner handcuffed him. "It's not true, I swear!"

"Lord Gerard did not return home that evening," Vicky said. "He fell asleep in the cottage belonging to Reverend Lesson. Just before sunrise, he awoke to find his sister murdered. By the time the baron made it to the home of Mr. Harding, the vicar had found the body of Miss Gerard and raised the alarm."

The glare Mr. Galpin gave Vicky should have had her bursting into flames. "She's lying! How could she know what happened if she wasn't there?"

Unruffled, Vicky said, "It was by your own admission that you spied on Mr. Haring. Yet, how could you have done that unless you had remained behind after your meeting? You waited for Mr. Haring to leave and then called on Miss Gerard again, hoping you could convince her to change her mind about you. She poured you a second glass of wine, which was customary every time you called, but you likely were not in a state of mind for socializing. Am I correct in saying so?"

"After all I did for her and she goes and chooses Faegan over me!" Mr. Galpin spat. "Yes, I returned. I wanted the truth, but all she shared were lies. So, I strangled her with a rope I found on the ground there." He lifted his chin to point toward the headstone.

"You will hang for this!" Lord Gerard said as he stormed toward Mr. Galpin, but the constable placed himself in his way. "By month's end, you will be dead!"

Vicky glanced around for Percy and was relieved to see him off in the far corner of the graveyard playing with a stick.

"Now that we have the culprit, Miss Parker," the baron growled, "where do I begin digging?"

Vicky smiled and clasped her hands in front of her. "But you have known the location of the treasure for a number of years, my lord.

It has been in front of you the entire time, yet you refused to see it."

Lord Gerard's face went as red as a beet. "What is this nonsense? I did not know its location."

"Ah, but you did. Your father returned from France with a treasure that no accountant would be able to fathom, and he was correct, for it had no value in the monetary sense. The treasure of which he spoke was love. It is no secret that he and your mother never loved one another, and while he was in France, he met a woman, whom he brought back to England with him. That was the reason he purchased flowers every time he left town."

"How can this be?" the baron bellowed, his face now a terrible scarlet. "That is the treasure? Love? I do not believe it! It must be something more."

Vicky shook her head and placed a hand on the tombstone beside them. "That woman is buried here, which explains why Reverend Lesson encountered your father here every week."

"That is true," the vicar replied with wide eyes. "He would come and then wander about, but he never revealed his reason for coming."

"And that is also why your father never revealed his secret to you, my lord," Vicky continued. "You would not have believed him any more than you do now. Your sister, however, did. That was why she held off marriage until she found a man she could love. A man with whom she could share the greatest treasure any could possess." She turned to Lord Faegan. "And she believed she had found that man with you, my lord, but as you explained to me, you do not trust in the idea of love. That is why you refused to share in the treasure she offered you."

Lord Faegan nodded. "Despite my impure intentions for trying to win her heart, she admitted that she had fallen in love with me. But I did not return her affections, or rather I could not allow myself to do so. Love is for fools, and I am in no way a fool. It is as you say, she revealed that love is the greatest treasure of all."

"That it is," Vicky said. "It cannot be purchased in any shop and is greater than any estate, title, or coin." She looked at James and smiled. "That is the treasure the former Baron Gerard possessed, and what he shared with Miss Mary Margaret Gerard. Sadly, that truth also led his daughter to her death."

"My father was a fool," Lord Gerard growled. "Love is a treasure? Tell me, where may I exchange love for food to eat? Or to pay off my debts? A complete and utter fool!" He pushed his way through the group of people gathered around them, nearly sending an older woman flying to the ground in his angry haste. Soon others followed after him.

Vicky sighed as James joined her.

"You did well," he said. "Are you glad it is over?"

She nodded. "I am relieved. I now wish for nothing more than to get Percy, and us, home."

Chapter Twenty-Four

The return journey was uneventful, Vicky simply enjoying the company of the two special men in her life. Percy had found another "friend" to bring home, a black stone that he held up to the window so it could "see the outside".

"'Is name's Edward Flemmin'."

Vicky chuckled. "That is a very specific name. Why did you choose it?"

"'Cause that's the name that was on the hea'stone where I found 'im. I figure 'es the man's ghost."

"Are you saying you have brought home someone's ghost?" James asked, clearly amused.

Percy nodded. "But 'e's promised to behave 'isself while 'e's 'ere. I told 'im 'e can only come if he don't bother no one, an' 'e said 'e won't. No 'auntin' us, not like Miss Brooks' ghost that 'aunts Miss Laura's hat shop."

When they returned to Wellington Street, the carriage came to a stop behind another. Vicky had forgotten that Miriam would be leaving, and she prayed for a smooth and uneventful farewell. Perhaps she should take the advice the former Lord Gerard had given his daughter and offer at least an olive branch. Miriam was an important part of James's life and therefore should be a part of hers, as well. Whether it led to even a friendship remained to be seen. What she could not allow was the woman overstepping her place, for what Vicky and James shared was between them.

As they entered the vestibule, Miriam called from the office, "I am in here, James."

James looked down at Vicky and smiled. "If you wish to join Andrew until she is gone, I will understand."

Vicky shook her head. "We can all say goodbye together," she said, taking Percy by the hand. "I would like to end her stay amicably."

When they entered the office, Miriam sat at the large desk once belonging to Vicky's father. She rose, although she did not look at Vicky. "I am saying my farewells now, as I will be leaving quite early in the morning tomorrow." She walked around the desk. "Although this has not been the most pleasant of visits, I will say no more on the matter." She embraced James and then turned to Vicky. "It is my hope that by the time I return you will no longer hate me."

Vicky smiled. "I do not hate you, and I am sorry you feel that way. I, too, had hoped for a better visit, but perhaps we can try again next time."

"Try again?" Miriam said with a snort. "Oh, Victoria, I will not play your manipulative games any longer."

"Vicky," James said, his voice stern.

Vicky's heart fell. So, he would side with his aunt until the very end. Perhaps there was no chance of reconciliation after all.

Yet, it was the words that followed that sent her heart soaring through the clouds, for he was addressing his aunt, not Vicky.

"She has asked that you call her Vicky."

"James, there is no need to use that tone with me. If you wish—"

"You may address her as Vicky or Miss Parker," James interrupted. "Or simply do not address her at all. The choice is yours, but you will no longer disrespect her by not adhering to her wishes."

Miriam took a startled step back. "She has warped your mind and turned you against me!"

"No, Aunt Miriam, she has not. It is you who created this problem."

Vicky leaned down and whispered in Percy's ear. "I suggest you take Mr. Flemming upstairs and introduce him to your other friends."

Percy gave her a grateful smile and hurried out of the room.

"When you took me into your home," James was saying, "it created some wonderful memories. However, there were other recollections, some about which I had forgotten, that have risen from the recesses of my mind. Memories of you belittling me. How often did you tell me that I was imperfect, that I was bound to fail? You sought to control my life at every turn, and if I chose to walk my own path, you ridiculed me for it. Oh, not necessarily outright, you are much too devious for that."

"I did no such thing," his aunt sputtered indignantly.

"Why do you think I chose to remain in London when you moved to the country? And why did I refuse a majority of your invitations to visit? It was because I realized that I am far worthier than you have ever been willing to admit. I simply do not wish to be spoken to that way again."

"Why, you ungrateful..." Miriam drew in a heavy breath and looked near apoplectic. "I have offered you everything, and yet you have no appreciation for what I have attempted to do for you. I have wanted nothing more than to better your life." She glanced at Vicky. "Your lives."

"That is what you seem to not understand," James said, maintaining that calm demeanor he always possessed. "Our life is perfect as it is. I had lost sight of that fact, but not anymore."

Vicky smiled. Never had she felt so loved, so important. Yet if she had learned anything during the past two weeks, one truth rose above them all.

"Miriam," she said as she took a step toward James's aunt, "I suspect that your reasons for helping us stem from your own pain."

Miriam straightened her back and pursed her lips. "My pain? What nonsense! My life is well enough, as it always has been."

"You are a woman who has had concerns that I am tempting your nephew, chosen maids who lack beauty, who spent many of her days in solitude at the dressmakers. And you are the same woman who feared for her nephew's wellbeing. You did all you could to see he did not become like his uncle, and you believe that the only way you could do that was to control his life. These actions are those of a woman who has been hurt."

James was frowning. "What do you mean? How is my aunt hurting? Would I have not noticed if she were?"

"No, you would not," Vicky replied. "So many women are able to pretend to be someone they are not. Is that not right, Miriam? There is no shame in admitting the truth."

"Now see here--" James began, but his aunt forestalled him.

"No, she is right," Miriam said, her eyes glistening with unshed tears. Your uncle had several affairs during our marriage, and his first was with a woman who worked at his factory. At first, I turned a blind eye; she was only one woman. Yet, soon late nights became overnights away, and I came to realize that I had failed in my duties as a wife. So often I wished I had done things differently, but by the time I reached that realization, it was far too late."

Vicky reached out a hesitant hand. "It was not your fault," she said. "You must understand that the choices were his, not yours. You admitted to me that you put everything into your marriage, but it was he who chose to ignore you."

Miriam sighed and shook her head. "Thank you," she said. Then she pulled her hand away and dabbed at her eyes with a handkerchief. "Thank you, Vicky, both of you. I am so sorry for the trouble I have caused. And you have given me much to consider." Then, to Vicky's surprise, she hugged her. "You are a woman so many dream of being. Perhaps you can teach me a few things."

Vicky smiled. "I would be happy to," she replied. "But I feel you have much to offer the world."

Miriam smiled and allowed James to hand in her into the carriage. As Vicky watched the vehicle pull away, she smiled at James, Percy between them. Never had her heart been so full. Two mysteries had been solved, and now that they no longer existed, Vicky looked forward to resuming her life.

"I'm goin' back inside," Percy said. "I left Mr. Flemming alone an' I don't wanna 'ave 'im causin' problems. Not that I think 'e will, but bein' as 'e's new an' all, I'd best keep a close eye on 'im."

"Go on then," Vicky said with a small laugh.

Once he was gone, James said, "Let us go to the office. I have something I would like to tell you."

Nodding, Vicky followed him inside.

James took her hands. "For what you endured the past two weeks, I am sorry. I became so consumed with what we lack that I lost sight of all we do have. I was no better than Lord Gerard if I am honest. Unlike him, however, I see the only treasure I need stands before me right now. You."

Vicky's heart fluttered with love. "And you, James, are my greatest treasure. In the future, if you wish to purchase a gift for me, make certain it is done in love alone, and I promise to accept it."

"You have my word," James replied. He placed a hand on her cheek. "Love truly is the greatest treasure." He leaned forward and pressed his lips to hers, and every worry, every concern she had endured the past weeks slipped away. The air around them seemed to disappear and an urgency filled her.

Later that evening as they sat around the dinner table, Vicky watched as Percy and James shared in stories. What a wonderful family they had created together, and it would only be better once she and James were wed.

Epilogue

"It has become apparent that we will soon need more accountants," James said as he sat hunched over the ledgers dedicated to Parker Accounting. Six weeks had passed since Miriam's departure, and Vicky and James had shared in many conversations, most discussing their future together, which included Percy. During those times, they laughed, the conversation free and uplifting.

It was times such as this, more serious discussions, that Vicky waited with great anticipation for that question she knew James would ask. What was taking him so long?

"If you are in agreement," James continued as he took her hand in his, "I believe it would be best if everyone was made aware of our standing."

Vicky's mouth went dry. "I would love that," she replied. Here it was, the moment when he would propose, and she had her answer prepared.

"Good," James said. "Then I must let you know that I would like—"

Andrew entered the room and then halted, his jaw dropping.

Vicky glanced at their intertwined hands and pulled back hers. "My hand was cold."

Her hand was cold? She wanted to run upstairs and hide. What made her say something so silly?

"It is all right, Miss Parker," Andrew said, a paper clutched in his hand. "I already know."

"Know what?" James asked, a blank look on his face.

"The...friendship." Andrew blushed as he dropped his gaze and held out the folded piece of parchment. "Percy dictated this and insisted it was important that I send it right away. Only, I am uncertain where to send it."

Vicky took the letter and unfolded it.

Dear Mr. Rabbit,

Miss Vicky and Mr. James are going to get married soon and they need children. Please deliver Miss Vicky five boys who like frogs.

Thank you,
Percy Lock

"I have no words," Andrew said in a voice so low, Vicky was barely able to hear him, "so perhaps I should remain silent."

James laughed. "Do you believe it would be appropriate to inform him of our plans now?"

"Most assuredly," Vicky said, smiling. "Andrew should be the first to know."

"We are planning to expand the firm and hire several more accountants!" James exclaimed.

Vicky sighed. She thought he would announce their engagement, joyous news Vicky wanted all in London to hear. But alas, today was another day not meant for proposals.

The question was, could she endure until that day came?

From the Author

Were you able to figure out the mystery? Check out the final installment of the Victoria Parker Regency Mysteries, *Duchesses, Diamonds, and Murder*.

If you enjoy Regency Romances that center around siblings, you will love my nine-part series that begins with a marriage of convenience in *Whispers of Light*.

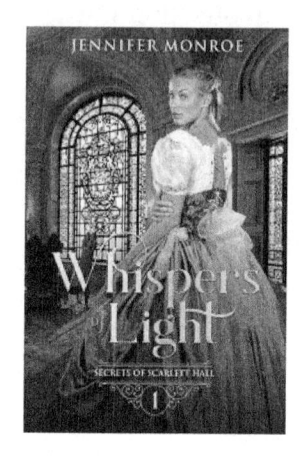

A Lady's Promise, the prequel to the Scarlett Hall series, tells of Miss Eleanor Parker's desire to wed the man she loves despite the wishes of an overbearing mother. Available for free from my website: www.jennifermonroeromance.com.

Printed in Great Britain
by Amazon